A Special Half-Price Invitation for New Subscribers

Since it began publishing in 1963, *The New York Review of Books* has provided remarkable variety and intellectual excitement. Every other week the world's best writers and scholars address themselves to discerning readers who represent something important in America... people who know that the widest range of subjects—art, literature, politics, science, history, music, education—will be discussed with wit, clarity, and brilliance.

And now we're offering a special invitation for new subscribers:

■ **21 issues.** You'll receive a full year's subscription of 21 issues for just $22.95. You pay only $1.15 a copy instead of the $2.95 per issue you would pay at the newsstand. That's nearly 50% off the subscription price and over 60% off the newsstand price.

■ **A Free Book.** With your paid subscription to *The New York Review,* you'll receive a 290-page softcover *Anthology* commemorating our first 30 years. The *Anthology,* a $7.95 value, includes essays originally published in *The Review* about some of the most important political and cultural events, written by Susan Sontag, Gore Vidal, Oliver Sacks, Andrei Sakharov, and 13 others.

■ **A risk-free guarantee.** If you are unhappy with your subscription, you may cancel and we will refund any unused portion of your subscription cost, at any time. Whatever you decide, the *Anthology* is yours to keep, as our gift to you.

Why not enter your subscription today, and start enjoying all of its benefits?

- -

The New York Review of Books

Please return this coupon to: Subscriber Service Dept., PO Box 420380, Palm Coast FL 32142-0380

Please enter my subscription to *The New York Review of Books* for a full year, 21 issues, at the special introductory price of $22.95, a saving of almost 50% off the regular subscription rate. With my paid subscription, I will also receive the *Anthology* at no extra charge.

Name _____ A4EH1M

Address _____

City _____ State _____ Zip _____

❑ $22.95 enclosed.* Or charge my ❑ Am Ex ❑ MasterCard ❑ Visa ❑ Send bill

Credit Card Number

Expiration Date: M/Y_____ Signature _____

☏ **For faster service on credit card orders, fax to: (212) 586-8003**

FREE with this offer!

* *Check or money order made payable to The New York Review of Books in US Dollars drawn on a US bank. Offer good for one year subscription for new subscribers within the US only. May not be used for gift subscriptions. Please allow 6 to 8 weeks for receipt of your first issue.*

MOVIE
XTRAS
NEEDED
10) 659-6233

GRAND STREET

Hollywood

49

Front and back cover: William Eggleston, *Untitled*, 1994

"The World is Round" is adapted from *The World is Round* by Iva Pekárková, translated by David Powelstock, to be published in July by Farrar, Straus & Giroux. Translation copyright © 1994 by David Powelstock. All rights reserved.

"Essay on the Jukebox" is adapted from *The Jukebox and Other Essays on Storytelling* by Peter Handke, translated by Ralph Manheim and Krishna Winston, to be published in August by Farrar, Straus & Giroux. Copyright © 1994. All rights reserved.

Grand Street is set in ITC New Baskerville by Crystal Graphics, Houston, Tex., and printed by Wetmore and Company, Houston, Tex. Color separations and halftones are by Typografiks, Inc., Houston, Tex.

Grand Street (ISBN 1-885490-00-3) is published quarterly by Grand Street Press (a project of the New York Foundation for the Arts, Inc., a not-for-profit corporation), 131 Varick Street, #906, New York, N.Y. 10013. Contributions and gifts to Grand Street Press, a project of the New York Foundation for the Arts, Inc., are tax-deductible to the extent allowed by law. This publication is made possible, in part, by a grant from the National Endowment for the Arts.

Second-class postage paid at New York, N.Y., and additional mailing offices. Postmaster: Please send address changes to *Grand Street* Subscription Service, Dept. GRS, P.O. Box 3000, Denville, N.J. 07834.

Subscription orders and address changes should be addressed to *Grand Street* Subscription Service, Dept. GRS, P.O. Box 3000, Denville, N.J. 07834. Subscriptions are $30 a year (four issues). Foreign subscriptions (including Canada) are $40 a year, and must be payable in U.S. funds. Single-copy price is $10 ($12.99 in Canada). To subscribe by phone or in case of subscription inquiries, please call (800) 783-4903.

Grand Street is distributed to the trade by D.A.P./Distributed Art Publishers, 636 Broadway, 12th floor, New York, N.Y. 10012, Tel: (212) 473-5119, Fax: (212) 673-2887, and to newsstands only by B. DeBoer, Inc., 113 E. Centre St., Nutley, N.J. 07110 and Fine Print Distributors, 6448 Highway 290 E., Austin, Tex. 78723.

GRAND STREET

Editor

Jean Stein

Managing Editor

Deborah Treisman

Art Editor

Walter Hopps

Poetry Editor

Erik Rieselbach

Designer

Don Quaintance

Assistant Editor

Howard Halle

Production Assistant

Elizabeth Frizzell

Editorial Assistant

Alystyre Julian

Administrative Assistant

Lisa Brodus

Copy Editor

Kate Norment

Interns

Isaac Bowers

James R. Garfield

Consulting Editor

Kristine McKenna

Contributing Editors

Hilton Als, Anne Doran, Morgan Entrekin, Gary Fisketjon,
Raymond Foye, Jonathan Galassi, Andrew Kopkind, Jane Kramer,
Olivier Nora, Edward W. Said, Robert Scheer, Elisabeth Sifton, Jean Strouse,
Jeremy Treglown, Katrina vanden Heuvel, Gillian Walker, Drenka Willen

Publishers

Jean Stein & Torsten Wiesel

CONTENTS

READY OR NOT

HERE I COME !!!

Blood Lust Snicker Snicker in Wide Screen

On March 17, 1994 I visited writer/director Quentin Tarantino at the Los Angeles house where he was editing his new film, Pulp Fiction, *a trilogy of stories set in contemporary Hollywood whose cast includes John Travolta, Bruce Willis, Uma Thurman, and Christopher Walken. While his staff had lunch, we talked and took pictures.*

—Dennis Hopper

DENNIS HOPPER: I heard one story, I don't know how true it is, that you started out in a video store.

QUENTIN TARANTINO: Yeah, uh huh. Well, it's funny. Actually I started out as an actor. I studied acting for six years—for three years with the actor James Best, then for three years with Alan Garfield. That's been my only formal training. I never went to film school or anything like that. And *then*—I was right at the point, after studying acting for years and years and years, when it comes time to actually go out and start trying to get a career—I suddenly realized that I really wanted to be a filmmaker, because I really was very different from all the kids in my acting class. I was always focused on the movies, I knew a lot about them and that was always my love. They all wanted to work with Robert DeNiro or Al Pacino—and I would have loved to work with them too—but what I really wanted was to work with the directors. I wanted to work with Francis Ford Coppola. I wanted to work with Brian De Palma and I would have learned Italian to work with Dario Argento.

So at a certain point I kind of realized that I didn't want to just *appear* in movies. I wanted the movies to be mine. And so right when I should have started trying to get an acting career going, I completely changed focus. In the meantime, the only thing I could do was get a job at this video store because of my knowledge of movies. And it ended up being like my college, all right. It's not that I learned so much about movies when I was there—they hired me because I was, you know, a movie geek—but it stopped me from having to work for a living, basically. I could just work at this place and talk about movies all day long and recommend movies all day long. And I got really comfortable. Too comfortable, as a matter of fact. It actually ruined me for ever having any real job because it just became like a big clubhouse.

DH: Where was this?

QT: In Manhattan Beach.

DH: How long were you there? How old are you now?

QT: I'm thirty-one. And I think I was twenty-two when I first started working there. But I got my college experience at that video store, you know. Not because I learned so much—I don't think you learn that much in college—it's the experience that matters. You're kind of breaking away and hanging out with a group of people, doing everything together and just screwing off.

DH: And you had access to all those films.

QT: Yeah, oh, that was the terrific part about it. I'd seen a lot of them already, but the thing was that I could watch them over and over again. We had a big-screen TV and we watched films *all day long* in the store. And I'd always put on stuff that I wasn't supposed to put on—you weren't supposed to put on stuff that had nudity or a lot of swear words, you know. But I was watching *Fingers* in the store. And *Ms. 45*, and wild stuff, Roger Corman women-in-prison movies. People would say, "What's this?" "Oh, that's Pam Grier."

Also, because I knew a lot about films and everything, if I wanted to see something, I would buy it. I've been collecting videos since videos came out. And so my collection was able to completely enlarge.

DH: So *Zatoichi: The Blind Swordsman*, all those Japanese films, did you already have a knowledge of them?

QT: Yeah. Most of the stuff I already had a knowledge of before, but I was able to completely indulge myself. And more important than that, I kind of fancied myself the Pauline Kael of the store. People would come in and I would kind of hold court with them. Eventually—and this was great for the first three years, and a major drag the last two years—people would come in and just say, "What do I want to see today, Quentin?" And I'd walk them through it: "Well, this is *Straight Time*, it's with Dustin Hoffman, it's one of the greatest crime movies ever made," and so on.

I remember—this is really weird—I created a following for Eric Rohmer in Manhattan Beach and the South Bay area. We had all of his films on video. So people would come up to me with *Pauline at the Beach*, or something—because they had those sexy boxes, you know—and ask, "How is this?" And I would feel I had to indoctrinate them on Eric Rohmer. "Well, he's a director you have to get used to. The thing is, actually, I like his films." "Well, are they comedy or are they drama?" "Well, they're not dramas, they're comedies but they're not really very funny, all right? You watch them and they're just lightly amusing, you know? You might smile once an hour, you know? But you have to see one of them, and if you kind of like that one, then you should see his other ones, but you need to see one to see if you like it." The same with Bresson.

DH: Or Satyajit Ray.

QT: Yeah, exactly. But in particular with Eric Rohmer. So I noticed that they'd rent *Full Moon in Paris* or *Pauline at the Beach*, and then they'd come back and get another one. And, pretty soon, all of our Rohmer movies were doing really, really well. But I could never rent them without giving that preamble. Because if they didn't know what to expect, it's conceivable that somebody just renting something for that Saturday afternoon would think, "What the hell is this?" and flip it off.

DH: I was trying to think about this phenomenon that's happening now—at least I see it happening—the new wave of violence in movies. I was thinking of names for it last night. And I thought of

"Blood Lust Snicker Snicker in Wide Screen." I don't really know what to call it, but you know what I mean. Could you expound on that a little? What do you think is happening right now? I see you as the forerunner of this. And certainly Sean Penn's films fall into this category.

QT: And Roger Avary's *Killing Zoe*.

DH: The one you produced? Right, exactly. I mean, there seem to be a lot of them. Even the *El Mariachi*'s. It's almost like a school of young filmmakers who are all doing this on their own. It's like the Abstract Expressionists—they didn't all get together and say, "Hey, let's paint abstractly." It was the next step on the ladder of evolution, and it's obviously coming out of the history of film and society and into a new thing. It's not film noir.

QT: No, it's not. I mean, I've thought a lot about this because it was so weird. It was like when I came out with *Reservoir Dogs* in '92, there just happened to be kind of an explosion of this kind of movie. I mean, I'm doing *Dogs* and Rémy Belvaux and André Bonzel are doing *Man Bites Dog* at the same time, a complete planet away, each of us not knowing that the other one exists. Yet now we're both finished and I was at more festivals with *Man Bites Dog* than any other film.

DH: It was at the Yubari Festival in Japan.

QT: Oh, yeah, but before that I was at four different festivals with it and it was something amazing. I mean, the films were polar opposites, they were different, but they fit into the same thing.

Apparently when Sergio Leone came out with his spaghetti westerns, they were very criticized for their violence. And his response at the time was something to the effect of, "Well, you know, I get that a lot in America but, oddly enough, Italians don't mind it. You see, Italians tend to laugh at violence. They don't take violence seriously."

Now, actually, the only people in America that take that attitude are black people. They don't let the violence affect them at all.

DH: Well, some of us others too . . .

QT: Yeah. But that's not the largest percentage. They can hoot and they can holler, you know, and kind of enjoy it for its own sake.

DH: How did you and Roger Avary meet?

QT: He worked at the video store with me. And he wrote the "Gold Watch" story in *Pulp Fiction*.

DH: Yes, oh, he did? That's incredible.

QT: Well, we co-wrote it. I wrote that monologue. But the whole boxer story was Roger's original idea.

I've never gotten that analytical about it myself, but, in a way—and this might be too pretentious—what we're reacting to in our movies is the fact that we see a lot of action films and we like them and we respond to them, but more often than not we're disappointed by them. They stop too short. And when I say they stop too short, I don't mean in terms of gore. I could care less about that—and they're pretty sufficient when it comes to that. But they stop too short in terms of balls, or even brutality, when the characters would in truth *be* brutal.

Oddly enough, novels don't fall short. If Charles Willeford or Elmore Leonard or Jim Thompson decides that the truth of the character should be that he blows a guy away even when he doesn't have a gun in his hand just because he's mad at him—if that's the truth of where he's coming from, that's the truth of where he's coming from. And I kind of get off on that, because I've been starved for it for the last ten years.

So when we get a chance to make our films, we don't want to wimp out; we don't want to disappoint ourselves. We've got a chance to make the movie that we've always been wanting to see and haven't been able to—except for a few stray examples. And almost all of those stray examples weren't recognized at the time. I'm always fighting to defend them. *Blue Velvet* was completely recognized and people looked up to that 100 percent. But, as far as I'm concerned, *King of New York* is better than *GoodFellas*. That is about as pure a vision as you're going to imagine. I mean, that's exactly what Abel Ferrara wanted to do his entire career. It has the polish and the artistry of a pure vision and, at the same time, it's just *full on out* action. When I see stuff like that, my response isn't to go, "ooh," my response is to laugh out loud.

It's like when Roger showed me the rough cut of *Killing Zoe* and I just howled through the whole damn movie. Until he doesn't want us to howl anymore—all the stuff with the old lady, when he's got the gun in her mouth, that's kind of funny, leading up to the point when he actually kills her, and that's not funny at all.

So when I see extreme violence in movies—or like, forget violence, *brutality*, all right, in movies—when it's done the way we're doing it, I tend to find it funny.

DH: Yes, yes.

QT: I think it's humorous, but it's not all one big joke. I want the work to have complexity. So it's hah-hah-hah, hah-hah-hah, hah-hah-hah, until I don't want you to laugh at all.

DH: So it's hah-hah-hah, ouch.

QT: Yes, exactly. And then you might even have to think about why you were laughing. And then I want to try to get you to start laughing again. The thing that I am really proud of in the torture scene in *Dogs* with Mr. Blonde, Michael Madsen, is the fact that it's truly funny up until the point that he cuts the cop's ear off. While he's up there doing that little dance to "Stuck in the Middle With You," I pretty much defy anybody to watch and not enjoy it. He's enjoyable at it, you know?

DH: Oh, yeah.

QT: He's cool. And then when he starts cutting the ear off, that's not played for laughs. The cop's pain is not played like one big joke, it's played for real. And then after that when he makes a joke, when he starts talking in the ear, that gets you laughing again. So now you've got his coolness and his dance, the joke of talking into the ear and the cop's pain, they're all tied up together. And that's why I think that scene caused such a sensation, because you don't know how you're supposed to feel when you see it.

DH: I saw it in Paris. Julian Schnabel took me to see it. He said, "You've got to see this movie." And Harvey Keitel had sent the script at one point for me to be in it.

QT: Right, to play Mr. Pink.

DH: I know. I loved it and I wanted to do it, but I had to do something else. So I went to see it with Julian, and it was *wild* seeing it in Paris, being an American, watching the film with the French. They were reacting and it was wonderful—and *packed*.

QT: It did great there. They totally got it. And it was like fun for me because when it comes to *Dogs*, in particular, the filmmaker that most inspired me was Jean-Pierre Melville.

DH: Oh, yeah.

QT: That's why a lot of us guys just like responded so much to the cinema coming out of Hong Kong—because they didn't have the rules and the bullshit that we were seeing in American action films. Boom, they'd just go for it, you know.

It's like I keep using the movie *Patriot Games* as an example of an uptight American action movie: It's supposed to be a revenge movie, all right, and as far as I'm concerned, if you're going to make a revenge movie, you've got to let the hero get revenge. There's a purity in that. You can moralize after the fact all you want, but people paid seven dollars to see it. So you set it up and the lead guy gets screwed over. And then, you want to see him kill the bad guys—with his bare hands, if possible. They've got to pay

for their sins. Now, if you want to, like, deal with morality after that, that's fine, but you've got to give me what I paid for. If you're going to invite me to a dance, you've gotta let me dance.

But the thing that is very unique, I mean, that is very indicative of American films, in *Patriot Games*, is the fact that the bad guy actually had a legitimate reason to want revenge against Harrison Ford. He caused the death of his brother. So he actually had a legitimate reason to create a vendetta against him. But the studio was so scared that we would even identify with the bad guy *that much*—to the point of understanding his actions—that they turned him into a psychopath. I never thought that he was a psychopath, and it took legitimacy away from what he was doing.

Then he bothers Harrison Ford so much that now Harrison Ford wants revenge. So you've got these two guys who both want revenge, which is an interesting place to be. But then they get into this stupid fight on this boat, and they do the thing that my friends and I despised the most: Harrison Ford hits the guy and he falls on an anchor and it kills him. And it's like you can hear a committee thinking about this and saying, "Well, he killed him with his own hands, but he didn't really mean to kill him, you know, so he can go back to his family, and his daughter, and his wife and still be an okay guy. He caused the death but it was kind of accidental." And as far as I'm concerned, the minute you kill your bad guy by having him fall on something, you should go to movie jail, all right. You've broken the law of good cinema. So I think that that is a pretty good analogy for where some of these new, relentlessly violent movies are coming from.

DH: Right. Well, there's a long history of these films. But they're taking a new approach and I'm very happy about it. What was that film I saw the other night with Gary Oldman?

QT: Oh, *Romeo is Bleeding.*

DH: I laughed straight through that movie, I loved it. I came out of the theater and I said, "Man, *this* is entertainment. If this film doesn't make it, I'm in deep shit." And I loved your movie the other night, your new film, *Pulp Fiction.* I mean, when Travolta is talking to the kid in the back seat, and then just blows his head off . . . it's outrageous. All the acting and the switches and the changes in the writing are just so wonderful.

QT: I guess if you're going to draw a parallel to the kind of comedy that's coming out in *Pulp Fiction*, I guess it's actually not very dissimilar to Monty Python—except that it's ridiculous in a more realistic way. You know, in *The Holy Grail* when the guy says, "Do you want to fight about it?" and the other guy cuts off his left arm, and the first guy still says, "Fight me," so he cuts off his right arm. And he still says, "Come on, it's a mere flesh wound, fight me, you coward!" So he cuts him in half and he *still* says, "Yeah I'll fight you, I'll take you on."

DH: It has all that, but then it has a reality to it that takes you to another place where you say, you know, this does really happen on some level, somewhere.

QT: See, to me, that's where the humor comes in, in particular in the third story in the movie. It deals with the reality of, okay they've accidentally shot this guy in this car, and now the car's covered with blood. They've got to deal with that. They're going to get picked up by the cops. They're in the Valley and the cops are all over the place there.

DH: They've got to get the brains and the blood out of the car— Harvey Keitel comes to do the clean-up, and they throw a party because they only have forty minutes to get it cleaned up.

QT: Before his wife comes home.

DH: Well, I feel that right now you're one of the top five young filmmakers. You remind me a lot of Francis [Ford Coppola] when he was young and excited and writing and creating. It was great to act your words, man.

QT: Well, as far as I'm concerned, you know, you and Chris [Walken] together in that scene in *True Romance*, that should go into a time capsule for future generations to look at.

I remember after Roger typed up *True Romance* for me, and we knew you lived in Venice, and we knew your house, we drove by a couple of times and we thought about. . . . Well, we were too embarrassed by the idea of knocking on the door and putting it in your hands and saying, "Hey, would you like to direct this?" So we talked about the idea of just like throwing it at your house.

DH: Well, if you have any more of those—throw 'em. *(Laughter.)*

QT: One of your performances that's one of my favorites—it's a wacky, kooky performance—is in *The Glory Stompers*. I *loved* you in that. You know, that *is* the beginning of you as Frank Booth in *Blue Velvet* right there.

DH: *Glory Stompers* is the American International Pictures movie which, actually, I ended up directing. That was my first directorial job because the director had a nervous breakdown.

QT: No, really? I'm a big biker movie fan anyway. But *The Glory Stompers* is really cool, because it looks like you're improvising it throughout the whole thing.

DH: Oh, yeah. I drove the guy to a nervous breakdown and then I took over the picture.

QT: You have this one line that's just *so* fucking funny in it: when you're fighting this guy, you beat him up, and then you look around and say, "Anybody else got anything else to say? Turn it on, man, just turn it on." *(Laughter.)*

DH: Well, thank you, man, because I know you're right in the middle of editing.

QT: No, this was my break. I'm honored that you wanted to do this.

GEORGANNE DEEN

THE TAKE OF THE TOWN

A private moment captured in the Ladies Lounge of Hollywood Moguls.

The Single-minded Pursuit of More

THE WHEEL OF MISFORTUNE

MATCH the PEOPLE with the REASONS
Why they Couldn't Get in the VIPER ROOM

☐ OVER-DRESSED

☐ WEARING FAKE GIORGIO

☐ UNDER THE VOLCANO

☐ WEARING FAKE TATTOOS

Weeping Women
Lena carries dark + painful secrets
Lisa's mother has gone nuts +
there's no one to take care of her but Lisa (who's broke)
Trudy hasn't had sex in 9 mos + she hates herself.
Jan won't be having any children

Eugenia doesn't know what the fuck she's doing wrong

P.M.S.

Judy's roommate told her to get out + she's broke

Tina Didn't get the Part

Elenore has a voice in her head telling her her life is Bogus

of Hollywood

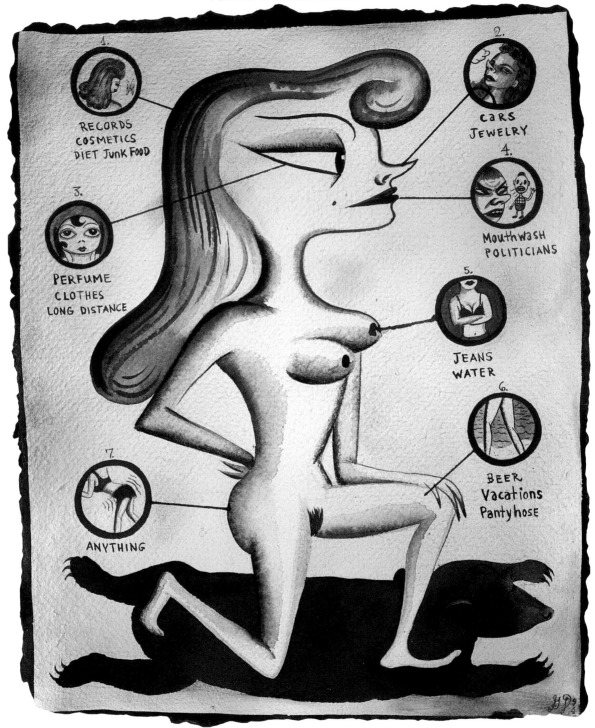

MODEL

ACTRESS

CONNOISSEUR

SPECIAL ISSUE

Hollywood Collectors

MORE DAZZLING THAN THE ART THEY BUY?

If you climb the hill above Georganne Deen's rented bungalow to just the right spot, on a day that isn't too jaundiced with smog, and sight along one of the narrow side yards between the little stucco houses and garages, you can catch a glimpse of HOLLYWOOD.

HOLLYWOOD, all caps, in white block letters, is a sign, not a place. It is an unspecific symbol—abstract, unadulterated, universal. There are other Hollywoods, more heavily laden symbols: Hollywood the cutthroat industry, Hollywood the sequined illusion, even Hollywood the city of nasty streets you wouldn't walk alone, of mansions-to-die-for perched in the hills.

Georganne Deen's Hollywood is at once more personal and more generic. The special effects in her pictures aside, her Hollywood may not be in California. More likely, it's in some lover-forsaken corner of some other city somewhere. Perhaps it's in Fort Worth, where the mother who confessed she'd "climb a flight of stairs to tell a lie" still lives.

Deen's Hollywood is populated almost exclusively by women ("the men don't matter *at all*," she says). It is the place where bulimia got its start, and battered wives force themselves to live, and bad-hair days are the norm—where the self-abuse of trying to live a fantasy as a real girl-woman catches up. Deen's art is one of rejection, in a style purloined from men (her brothers' hot-rod books introduced her to Big Daddy Roth and Robert Williams early on). Frederick's of Hollywood catalogues continue to be a major influence.

A dropout from some good schools—East Texas State in 1974, CalArts in 1980—Deen today enjoys notoriety as an underground comix artist and magazine illustrator. The attention paid her by the fine arts establishment has been halting, however, consisting of regular inclusion in solo and group exhibitions at alternative galleries, but arm's-length treatment by collectors and critics. It is hard to know where to cubbyhole an angry cartoonist and her impassioned spewings. Deen is far from an "Outsider" artist ("I *wish*," she says. "Maybe when I'm institutionalized.") But she nevertheless shares with those naive visual geniuses a propensity for tactless truth and untamed ingenuity. She also shares their tendency toward autobiography. "All of the women," she confides, "are me."

Yet the image she offers of a woman's self-inflicted harm—damage in response to unsatisfiable cultural expectations—is a bit like the glimpse of the Hollywood sign one gets from her neighborhood. Not abstract, of course, and certainly not unadulterated, but all too universal.

—Charles Desmarais

Hard-Boiled

The R.V.s parked in the Comstock lot radiated heat,
waves of it.
       Reminds me of El Centro, Gladys said.
One June it was so hot you could only pick up two stations
on the radio.
        But south of town you could still make out patches
of snow on the higher peaks over toward Steamboat and Virginia City.

Gladys had the sort of face that belongs in magazines
where you're not supposed to notice the face.
          The hotel she found us
was one of those old brick affairs with a fancy cornice
and Nevada Gothic in the doors and windows.
Probably elegant once, it now felt more like the backdrop
for a Jim Thompson novel, one that will never be filmed.

The old guy at the front desk was a top classic fit as well
with the cowboy tie, suspenders, and tiny white mustache:
dapper, creased, and shiny to the tips of his pointy, black boots.
Everybody was out of central casting that week,
even the drifters lounging around outside the Mission
or that beat-up little bungalow called House of Hope.
So when Eddie took a shiv in his gut that night
in the parking lot of Mr. D's Backstage Club
we were into the plot, Gladys, the killer, and me,
whether we liked it or not.

My life's been a succession of Gladyses, I thought to myself,
watching her pore over the *Racing Form* hours on end,
smoking Chesterfields in her underwear.
                                      Late afternoons
she'd go catch the feature race at the Sports Parlor
in the Flamingo and commence with the gimlets.
Meanwhile, she might as well have been reading the Talmud
she was so still and engrossed, except when she butted her smokes
on Goofy's snout in the joke ashtray she won at some casino.

I found myself on a barstool later that evening
at Mr. D's next to a curiously solemn Englishman.
He smelled of prime rib, bourbon, and sweat and kept sticking
five-spots in the panties of a young blond who danced
dirty for him while he just sat there and sipped his whiskey.

Between songs you could hear the freeway in the distance.
He was one of those gruff, blocky, northern English,
working-class, who said *ruhf* (as in *bow-wow*) for *rough*.
You'd think he'd never seen a blond in her knickers before
the way he kept muttering—
                           Christ, you're buffed
(rhyming with *ruhf'd*), then something about a *chubby* he had *on*.

I decided to go outside and take some fresh air
when I ran into Lois, a high yellow gal from back East.
She was older than the others and used to know Gladys
from their Century 21 days over in Tahoe.
I checked out the giant billboard across the highway
with Sammy Davis and Roy Orbison look-alikes:
something about a forthcoming *Night of Stars.*

Dead stars, seemed like to me.
Lois knew I wasn't there for a couch dance.
Eddie and I go all the way back to lava lamps,
when we ran up and down the coast to Ensenada.
Lois would have been just a scowling kid then,
pitching pennies against a wall in Brooklyn.

The Southern Pacific began roaring past
along the top of a ridge a few blocks behind us,
pulling eighty carloads of coal from Utah.
I suddenly picked up a whiff of her perfume.
It reminded me a little too well of car freshener.
That was an instant before she fell into my arms,
dead as the smoked trout Gladys had for dinner
at the Basque place, along with about seven gimlets,
on an evening that now seemed a lifetime away.

Mr. Vertigo

I gave my first public performance on August 25, 1927, appearing as Walt the Wonder Boy for a one-show booking at the Pawnee County Fair in Larned, Kansas. It would be hard to imagine a more modest debut, but as things turned out, it came within an inch of being my swan song. It wasn't that I flubbed up the act, but the crowd was so raucous and mean-spirited, so filled with drunks and hooters, that if not for some quick thinking on the master's part, I might not have lived to see another day.

They'd roped off a field on the other side of the horticultural exhibits, out past the stalls with the prize-winning ears of corn and the two-headed cow and the six-hundred-pound pig, and I remember traveling for what seemed like half a mile before coming to a little pond with murky green water and white scum floating on top. It struck me as a woeful site for such a historic occasion, but the master wanted me to start small, with as little fuss and fanfare as possible. "Even Ty Cobb played in the bush leagues," he said, as we climbed out of Mrs. Witherspoon's car. "You have to get some performances under your belt. Do well here, and we'll start talking about the big time in a few months."

Unfortunately, there was no grandstand for the spectators, which made for a lot of tired legs and surly complaints, and with tickets going at ten cents a pop, the crowd was already feeling chiseled before I made my entrance. There couldn't have been more than sixty or seventy of them, a bunch of thick-necked hayseeds milling around in their overalls and flannel shirts—delegates from the First International Congress of Bumpkins. Half of them were guzzling bathtub hooch from little brown cough-syrup bottles and the other half had just finished theirs and were itching for more. When Master Yehudi stepped forward in his black tuxedo and silk hat to announce the world premiere of Walt the Wonder Boy, the wisecracks and heckling began. Maybe they didn't like his clothes, or maybe they objected to his Brooklyn-Budapest accent, but I'm certain it didn't help that I was wearing the worst costume in the annals of show business: a long white robe that made me look like some midget John the Baptist, complete with leather sandals and a hemp sash tied around my waist. The master had insisted on what he called an "otherworldly look," but I felt like a twit in that getup, and when I heard some clown yell at the top of his voice—"Walt the Wonder Girl"—I realized I wasn't alone in my sentiments.

If I found the courage to begin, it was only because of Aesop. I knew he was looking down on me from wherever he was, and I wasn't going to let myself fail him. He was counting on me to shine, and whatever that soused-up mob of fools might have thought of me, I owed it to my brother to give it the best shot I could. So I walked to the edge of the pond and went into my spread-arms-and-trance routine, struggling to shut out the catcalls and insults. I heard some oohs and ahs when my body rose off the ground—but dimly, only dimly, for I was already in a separate world by then, walled off from friend and foe alike in the glory of my ascent. It was the first performance I had ever given, but I already had the makings of a trooper, and I'm certain I would have won over the crowd if not for some birdbrain who took it upon himself to hurl a bottle in my direction. Nineteen times out of twenty, the projectile sails past me and no harm is done, but this was a day for flukes and long shots, and the damned thing clunked me square in the noggin. The blow addled my concentration (not to speak of rendering me unconscious), and before I knew which end was up, I was sinking like a bag of pennies to the bottom of the water. If the master hadn't been on his toes, diving in after me without bothering to shed his coat and tails, I probably would have drowned in that crummy mudhole, and that would have been the first and last bow I ever took.

So we left Larned in disgrace, hightailing it out of there as those bloodthirsty hicks pelted us with eggs and stones and watermelons. No one seemed to care that I'd almost died from that blow on the head, and they went on laughing as the good master rescued me from the drink and carried me to the safety of Mrs. W's car. I was still semidelirious from my visit to Davy Jones's locker, and I coughed and puked all over the master's shirt as he ran across the field with my wet body bouncing in his arms. I couldn't hear everything that was said, but enough reached my ears for me to gather that opinions about us were sharply divided. Some people took the religious view, boldly asserting that we were in league with the devil. Others called us fakes and charlatans, and still others had no opinion at all. They yelled for the pure pleasure of yelling, just glad to be part of the mayhem as they let forth with angry, wordless howls. Fortunately, the car was waiting for us on the other side of the roped-off area, and we managed to get inside before the rowdies caught up with us. A few eggs thudded against the rear window as we drove off, but no glass shattered, no shots rang out, and all in all I suppose we were lucky to escape with our hides intact.

We must have traveled two miles before either one of us found the courage to speak. We were out among the farms and pastures by then, tooling along a bumpy byway in our drenched and sopping clothes. With each jolt of the car, another spurt of pond water gushed from us and sank into Mrs. Witherspoon's deluxe suede upholstery. It sounds funny as I tell it now, but I wasn't the least bit tempted to laugh at the time. I just sat there stewing in the front seat, trying to control my temper and figure out what had gone wrong. In spite of his errors and miscalculations, it didn't seem fair to blame the master. He'd been through a lot, and I knew his judgment wasn't all it should have been, but it was my fault for going along with him. I never should have allowed myself to get sucked into such a half-assed, poorly planned operation. It was my butt on the line out there, and when all was said and done, it was my job to protect it.

"Well, partner," the master said, doing his best to crack a smile, "welcome to show biz."

"That wasn't no show biz," I said. "What happened back there was assault and battery. It was like walking into an ambush and getting scalped."

"That's the rough and tumble, kid, the give and take of crowds. Once the curtain goes up, you never know what's going to happen."

"I don't mean to be disrespectful, sir, but that kind of talk ain't nothing but wind."

"Oh ho," he said, amused by my plucky rejoinder. "The little lad's in a huff. And what kind of talk do you propose we engage in, Mr. Rawley?"

"Practical talk, sir. The kind of talk that'll stop us from repeating our mistakes."

"We didn't make any mistakes. We just drew a bum audience, that's all. Sometimes you get lucky, sometimes you don't."

"Luck's got nothing to do with it. We did a lot of dumb things today, and we wound up paying the price."

"I thought you were brilliant. If not for that flying bottle, it would have been a four-star success."

"Well, for one thing, I'd sincerely like to ditch this costume. It's about the awfullest piece of hokum I ever saw. We don't need no otherworldly trappings. The act's got enough of that already, and we don't want to confuse folks by dressing me up like some nancy-boy angel. It puts them off. It makes me look like I'm supposed to be better than they are."

"You *are* better, Walt. Don't ever forget that."

"Maybe so. But once we let them know that, we're sunk. They were against me before I even started."

"The costume had nothing to do with it. That crowd was stoned, pickled to the toe jam in their socks. They were so cross-eyed, not one of them even saw what you had on."

"You're the best teacher there is, master, and I'm truly grateful to you for saving my life today, but on this particular point, you're as wrong as any mortal man can be. The costume stinks. I'm sorry to be so blunt, but no matter how hard you yell at me, I ain't never wearing it again."

"Why would I yell at you? We're in this together, son, and you're free to express your opinions. If you want to dress another way, all you have to do is tell me."

"On the level?"

"It's a long trip back to Wichita, and there's no reason why we shouldn't discuss these things now."

"I don't mean to grumble," I said, jumping through the door he'd just opened for me, "but the way I see it, we ain't got a prayer unless we win them over from the get-go. These rubes don't like no fancy stuff. They didn't take to your penguin suit, and they didn't take to my sissy robe. And all that high-flown talk you pitched them at the start—it went right over their heads."

"It was nothing but gibberish. Just to get them in the mood."

"Whatever you say. But how's about we skip it in the future? Just keep it simple and folksy. You know, something like 'Ladies and gentlemen, I'm proud to present,' and then back off and let me come on. If you wear a plain old seersucker suit and a nice straw hat, no one will take offense. They'll think you're a friendly, good-hearted Joe out to make an honest buck. That's the key, the whole sack of onions. I stroll out before them like a little know-nothing, a wide-eyed farm boy dressed in denim overalls and a plaid shirt. No shoes, no socks, a barefoot nobody with the same geek mug as their own sons and nephews. They take one look at me and relax. It's like I'm a member of the family. And then, the moment I start rising into the air, their hearts fail them. It's that simple. Soften them up, then hit them with the whammy. It's bound to be good. Two minutes into the act, they'll be eating out of our hands like squirrels."

It took almost three hours to get home, and all during the ride I talked, speaking my mind to the master in a way I'd never done before. I covered everything I could think of—from costumes to venues, from ticket-taking to music, from show times to publicity—and he let me have my say. There's no question that he was impressed, maybe even a little startled by my thoroughness and strong opinions, but I was fighting for my life that afternoon, and it wouldn't have helped the cause to hold back and mince words. Master Yehudi had launched a ship that was full of holes, and rather than try to plug those holes as the water rushed in and sank us, I wanted to drag the thing back to port and rebuild it from the bottom up. The master listened to my ideas without interrupting or making fun of me, and in the end he gave in on most of the points I raised. It couldn't have been easy for him to accept his failure as a showman, but Master Yehudi wanted things to work as much as I did, and he was big enough to admit that he'd gotten us off on the wrong track. It wasn't that he didn't have a method, but that method was out of date, more suited to the corny prewar style he'd grown up with than to the jump and jangle of the new age. I was after something modern, something sleek and savvy and direct, and little by little I managed to talk him into it, to bring him around to a different approach.

Still, on certain issues he refused to fall in line. I was keen on taking the act to Saint Louis and showing off in front of my old hometown, but he nipped that proposition in the bud. "That's the most dangerous spot on earth for you," he said, "and the minute you go back there, you'll be signing your own death warrant. Mark my words. Saint Louis is bad medicine. It's a poison place, and you'll never get out of there alive." I couldn't understand his vehemence, but he talked like someone whose mind was set, and there was no way I could go against him. As it turned out, his words proved to be dead on the mark. Just one month after he spoke them to me, Saint Louis was hit by the worst tornado of the century. The twister shot through town like a cannonball from hell, and by the time it left five minutes later, a thousand buildings had been flattened, a hundred people were dead, and two thousand others lay writhing in the wreckage with broken bones and blood pouring from their wounds. We were on our way to Vernon, Oklahoma, by then, on the fifth leg of a fourteen-stop tour, and when I picked up the morning edition of the local rag and saw the pictures on the front page, I almost regurgitated my breakfast. I'd thought the master had lost his touch, but once again I'd sold him short. He knew things I would never know, he heard things no one else could hear, and not a man in the world could match him. If I ever doubt his words again, I told myself, may the Lord strike me down and scatter my corpse to the pigs. . . .

When we pulled into Redbird two days later, I was as keyed up as a jack-in-the-box and crazier than a monkey. It's going to work this time, I told myself. Yes sir, this is where it all begins. Even the name of the town struck me as a good omen, and since I was nothing if not superstitious in those days, it had a powerful effect on my spirits. Redbird. Just like my ball club in Saint Louis, my dear old chums the Cardinals.

It was the same act in a new set of clothes, but everything felt different somehow, and the audience took a shine to me the moment I came on—which was half the battle right there. Master Yehudi did his corn-pone spiel to the hilt, my Huck Finn costume was the last word in understatement, and all in all we knocked them dead. Six or seven women fainted, children screamed, grown men gasped in awe and disbelief. For thirty minutes I kept them spellbound, prancing and tumbling in midair, gliding my little body over the surface of a broad and sparkling lake, and then, at the end, pushing myself to a record height of four and a half feet before floating back to the ground and taking my bow. The applause was thunderous, ecstatic. They whooped and cried, they banged pots and pans, they tossed confetti into the air. This was my first taste of success, and I loved it, I loved it in a way I've never loved anything before or since.

Dunbar and Battiest. Jumbo and Plunketsville. Pickens, Muse, and Bethel. Wapanucka. Boggy Depot and Kingfisher. Gerty, Ringling, and Marble City. If this were a movie, here's where the calendar pages would start flying off the wall. We'd see them fluttering against a background of country roads and tumbleweed, and then the names of those towns would flash by as we followed the progress of the black Ford across a map of eastern Oklahoma. The music would be jaunty and full of bounce, a syncopated chug-chug to ape the noise of ringing cash registers. Shot would follow shot, each one melting into the other. Bushel baskets brimming with coins, roadside bungalows, clapping hands and stomping feet, open mouths, bug-eyed faces turned to the sky. The whole sequence would take about ten seconds, and by the time it was over, the story of that month would be known to every person in the theater. Ah, the old Hollywood razzmatazz. There's nothing like it for hustling things along. It may not be subtle, but it gets the job done.

So much for the quirks of memory. If I'm suddenly thinking about movies now, it's probably because I saw so many of them in the months that followed. After the Oklahoma triumph, bookings ceased to be a problem, and the master and I spent most of our time on the road, moving around from one backwater to another. We played Texas, Arkansas, and Louisiana, dipping farther and

farther south as winter came on, and I tended to fill in the dead
time between performances by visiting the local Bijou for a peek
at the latest flick. The master generally had business to take care
of—talking to fair managers and ticket sellers, distributing hand-
bills and posters around town, adjusting nuts and bolts for the
upcoming performance—which meant he seldom had time to go
with me. More often than not, I'd come back to find him alone
in the room, sitting in a chair reading his book. It was always the
same book—a battered little green volume that he carried with
him on all our travels—and it became as familiar to me as the
lines and contours of his face. It was written in Latin, of all things,
and the author's name was Spinoza, a detail I've never forgotten,
even after so many years. When I asked the master why he kept
studying that one book over and over again, he told me it was
because you could never get to the bottom of it. The deeper you
go, he said, the more there is, and the more there is, the longer it
takes to read it.

"A magic book," I said. "It can't never use itself up."

"That's it, squirt. It's inexhaustible. You drink down the wine,
put the glass back on the table, and lo and behold, you reach for
the glass again and discover it's still full."

"And there you are, drunk as a skunk for the price of one
drink."

"I couldn't have put it better myself," he said, suddenly turning from me and gazing out the window. "You get drunk on the
world, boy. Drunk on the mystery of the world."

Christ but I was happy out there on the road with him. Just
moving from place to place was enough to keep my spirits up, but
when you added in all the other ingredients—the crowds, the performances, the money we made—those first months were hands
down the best months I'd ever lived. Even after the initial excitement wore off and I grew accustomed to the routine, I still didn't
want it to stop. Lumpy beds, flat tires, bad food, all the rainouts
and lulls and boring stretches were as nothing to me, mere pebbles
bouncing off the skin of a rhinoceros. We'd climb into the Ford
and blow out of town, another seventy or hundred bucks stashed
away in the trunk, and then mosey on to the next whistle-stop,
watching the landscape roll by as we chewed over the finer points
of the last performance. The master was a prince to me, always

encouraging and counseling and listening to what I said, and he
never made me feel that I was one bit less important than he was.
So many things had changed between us since the summer, it was
as if we were on a new footing now, as if we'd reached some kind
of permanent equilibrium. He did his job and I did mine, and
together we made the thing work.

The stock market didn't crash until two years later, but the
Depression had already started in the hinterlands, and farmers
and rural folks throughout the region were feeling the pinch. We
came across a lot of desperate people on our travels, and Master
Yehudi taught me never to look down on them. They needed Walt
the Wonder Boy, he said, and I must never forget the responsibility
that need entailed. To watch a twelve-year-old do what only saints
and prophets had done before him was like a jolt from heaven,
and my performances could bring spiritual uplift to thousands
of suffering souls. That didn't mean I shouldn't make a bundle
doing it, but unless I understood that I had to touch people's
hearts, I'd never gain the following I deserved. I think that's why
the master started my career in such out-of-the-way places, such
a rinky-dink collection of forgotten corners and crevices on the
map. He wanted the word about me to spread slowly, for support
to begin from the ground up. It wasn't just a matter of breaking
me in, it was a way of controlling things, of making sure I didn't
turn out to be a flash in the pan.

Who was I to object? The bookings were organized in a sys-
tematic way, the turnouts were good, and we always had a roof
over our heads when we went to sleep at night. I was doing what I
wanted to do, and the feeling it gave me was so good, so exhilarat-
ing, I couldn't have cared less if the people who saw me perform
were from Paris, France, or Paris, Texas. Every now and then, of
course, we encountered a bump in the road, but Master Yehudi
seemed to be prepared for any and all situations. Once, for example, a truant officer came knocking on the door of our rooming
house in Dublin, Mississippi. "Why isn't this lad in school?" he
said to the master, pointing his long bony finger at me. There are
laws against this, you know, statutes, regulations, and so on and so
forth. I figured we were sunk, but the master only smiled, asked
the gentleman to step in, and then pulled a piece of paper from
the breast pocket of his coat. It was covered with official-looking

stamps and seals, and once the truant officer read it through, he tipped his hat in an embarrassed sort of way, apologized for the mixup, and left. God knows what was written on that paper, but it did the trick in one fast hurry. Before I could make out any of the words, the master had already folded up the letter and slipped it back into his coat pocket. "What does it say?" I asked, but even though I asked again, he never answered me. He just patted his pocket and grinned, looking awfully smug and pleased with himself. He reminded me of a cat who'd just polished off the family bird, and he wasn't about to tell me how he'd opened the cage.

From the latter part of 1927 through the first half of 1928, I lived in a cocoon of total concentration. I never thought about the past, I never thought about the future—only about what was happening now, the thing I was doing at this or that moment. On the average, we didn't spend more than three or four days a month in Wichita, and the rest of the time we were on the road, bee-lining hither and yon in the black Wondermobile. . . .

The whole operation had moved up a notch or two: larger towns for the performances, small hotels instead of rooming houses and guest cottages to flop our bones in, more stylish transportation. . . . And for the next few months I pulled out one stop after another, adding new wrinkles and flourishes to the act almost every week. I had grown so accustomed to the crowds by then, felt so at ease during my performances, that I was able to improvise as I went along, actually to invent and discover new turns in the middle of a show. In the beginning I had always stuck to the routine, rigidly following the steps the master and I had worked out in advance, but I was past that now, I had hit my stride, and I was no longer afraid to experiment. Locomotion had always been my strength. It was the heart of my act, the thing that separated me from every levitator who had come before me, but my loft was no better than average, a fair to middling five feet. I wanted to improve on that, to double or even triple that mark if I could, but I no longer had the luxury of all-day practice sessions, the old freedom of working under Master Yehudi's supervision for ten or twelve hours at a stretch. I was a pro now, with all the burdens and scheduling constraints of a pro, and the only place I could practice was in front of a live audience.

So that's what I did . . . and to my immense wonderment I
found that the pressure inspired me. Some of my finest tricks date
from that period, and without the eyes of the crowd to spur me
on, I doubt that I would have mustered the courage to try half the
things I did. It all started with the staircase number, which was the
first time I ever made use of an "invisible prop"—the term I later
coined for my invention. We were in upper Michigan then, and
smack in the middle of the performance, just as I rose to begin my
crossing of the lake, I caught sight of a building in the distance. It
was a large brick structure, probably a warehouse or an old factory,
and it had a fire escape running down one of the walls. I couldn't
help but notice those metal stairs. The sunlight was bouncing off
of them at just that moment, and they were gleaming with a frantic
kind of brightness in the late afternoon sun. Without giving the
matter any thought, I lifted one foot into the air, as if I were about
to climb a real staircase, and put it down on an invisible step; then
I lifted the other foot and put it down on the next step. It wasn't
that I felt anything solid in the air, but I was nevertheless going up,
gradually ascending a staircase that stretched from one end of the
lake to the other. Even though I couldn't see it, I had a definite
picture of it in my mind. To the best of my recollection, it looked
something like this:

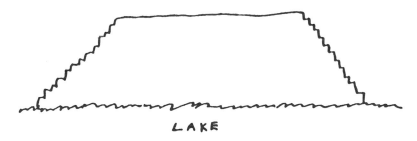

LAKE

At its highest point—the platform in the middle—it was roughly
nine and a half feet above the surface of the water—a good four
feet higher than I'd ever been before. The eerie thing was that I
didn't hesitate. Once I had that picture clearly in my mind, I knew
I could depend on it to get me across. All I had to do was follow
the shape of the imaginary bridge, and it would support me as if it
were real. A few moments later, I was gliding across the lake with
nary a hitch or a stumble. Twelve steps up, fifty-two steps across,

and then twelve steps down. The results were nothing less than perfect.

After that breakthrough, I discovered that I could use other props just as effectively. As long as I could imagine the thing I wanted, as long as I could visualize it with a high degree of clarity and definition, it would be available to me for the performance. That was how I developed some of the most memorable portions of my act: the rope-ladder routine, the slide routine, the seesaw routine, the high-wire routine, the countless innovations I was heralded for. Not only did these turns enhance the audience's pleasure, but they thrust me into an entirely new relationship with my work. I wasn't just a robot anymore, a wind-up baboon who did the same set of tricks for every show—I was evolving into an artist, a true creator who performed as much for his own sake as for the sake of others. It was the unpredictability that excited me, the adventure of never knowing what was going to happen from one show to the next. If your only motive is to be loved, to ingratiate yourself with the crowd, you're bound to fall into bad habits, and eventually the public will grow tired of you. You have to keep testing yourself, pushing your talent as hard as you can. You do it for yourself, but in the end it's this struggle to do better that most endears you to your fans. That's the paradox. People begin to sense that you're out there taking risks for them. They're allowed to share in the mystery, to participate in whatever nameless thing is driving you to do it, and once that happens, you're no longer just a performer, you're on your way to becoming a star. In the fall of 1928, that's exactly where I was: on the brink of becoming a star.

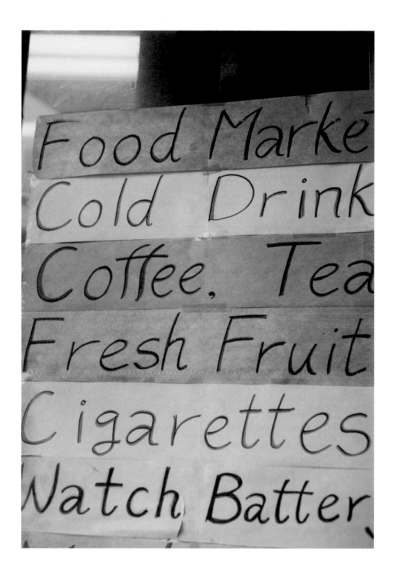

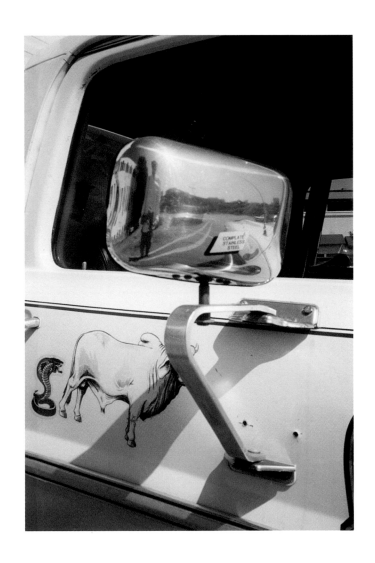

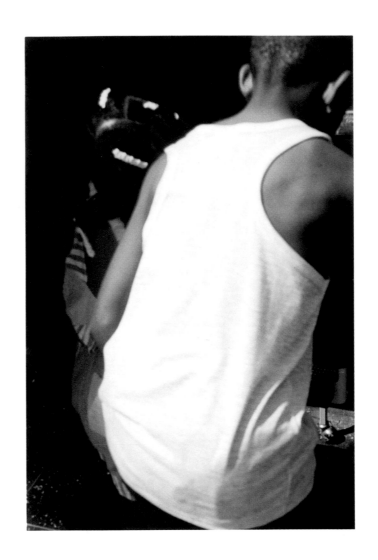

Columbia Pictures Presents

Peter Sellers · George C. Scott

in Stanley Kubrick's

Dr. Strangelove

Or: How I Learned To Stop Worrying And Love The Bomb

also starring
Sterling Hayden · Keenan Wynn · Slim Pickens and introducing Tracy Reed Screenplay by Stanley Kubrick, Peter George & Terry Southern
(as Miss Foreign Affairs.)

Based on the book "Red Alert" by Peter George · Produced and Directed by Stanley Kubrick

Strangelove Outtake:
Notes from the War Room

1962. It was a death-gray afternoon in early December and the first snow of the New England winter had just begun. Outside my window, between the house and the banks of the frozen stream, great silver butterfly flakes floated and fluttered in the failing light. Beyond the stream, past where the evening mist had begun to rise, it was possible, with a scintilla of imagination, to make out the solemnly moving figures in the Bradbury story about the Book People; in short, a magical moment—suddenly undone by the ringing of a telephone somewhere in the house, and then, closer at hand, my wife's voice in a curious singsong:

"It's big Stan Kubrick on the line from Old Smoke."

I had once jokingly referred to Kubrick, whom I had never met but greatly admired, as "big Stan Kubrick" because I liked the ring and lilt of it. "Get big Stan Kubrick on the line in Old Smoke," I had said, "I'm ready with my incisive critique of *Killer's Kiss*." And my wife, not one to be bested, had taken it up.

"Big Stan Kubrick," she repeated, "on the line from Old Smoke."

"Don't fool around," I said. I knew I would soon be on the hump with Mr. Snow Shovel and I was in no mood for her brand of tomfoolery.

"I'm not fooling around," she said. "It's him all right, or at least his assistant."

I won't attempt to reconstruct the conversation; suffice to say he told me he was going to make a film about "our failure to understand the dangers of nuclear war." He said that he had thought of the story as a "straightforward melodrama" until this morning, when he "woke up and realized that nuclear war was too outrageous, too fantastic to be treated in any conventional manner." He said he could only see it now as "some kind of hideous joke." He told me that he had read a book of mine which contained, as he put it, "certain indications" that I might be able to help him with the script.

I later learned the curious genesis of all this: during the '50s I was friends with the English writer Jonathan Miller. I knew him for quite a while before I discovered that he was a doctor—of the sort who could write you a prescription for something like Seconal— at which point I beseeched him to become my personal physician and perhaps suggest something for my chronic insomnia. To encourage his acceptance, I gave him a copy of my recently published novel, *The Magic Christian*, which had been favorably reviewed in the *Observer* by the great English novelist Henry Green. Miller was impressed, at least enough to recommend it to his friend Peter Sellers. Peter liked it to the improbable degree that he went straight to the publisher and bought a hundred copies to give to his friends. One such friend, as luck would have it, was Stanley Kubrick.

At Shepperton Studios in London, Kubrick had set up his "Command Post" in a snug office that overlooked two wintering lilac bushes and, poetically enough, the nest of an English nightingale. Next to his big desk, and flush against it, stood an elegant wrought-iron stand that resembled a pedestal, and on top of the stand, at desk level, was one of the earliest, perhaps the very first, of the computerized "chess-opponents," which they had just begun to produce in West Germany and Switzerland. It was a sturdy, workmanlike model, black with brushed-metal lettering across the front:

GRAND MASTER LEVEL

"I have perfected my endgame," Kubrick said, "to such a degree that I can now elude the stratagems of this so-called opponent," he gave a curt nod toward the computer, "until the proverbial cows come home. . . . Would that I could apply my newly acquired skill," he went on, "vis-à-vis a certain Mo Rothman at Columbia Pix."

Mo Rothman, I was to learn, was the person Columbia Pictures had designated executive producer on the film, which meant that he was the bridge, the connection, the *interpreter*, between the otherwise incomprehensible artist and the various moneybags incarnate who were financing the film. As to whether or not the "streetwise" Mo Rothman was a good choice for this particular project, I believe the jury is still out. Once, when Kubrick was out of the office, Rothman insisted on giving me the following message:

"Just tell Stanley," he said in a tone of clamor and angst, "that New York does *not* see anything *funny* about the end of the world!" And then added, not so much as an afterthought as a simple Pavlovian habit he'd acquired, "as we know it."

I realized he had no idea whom he was talking to, so I took a flyer. "Never mind New York," I said with a goofy inflection, "What about Gollywood?"

This got a rise out of him like a shot of crystal meth.

"*Gollywood?*" he said loudly. "Who the hell *is* this?"

The Corporate, that is to say, studio reasoning about this production affords an insight as to why so many such projects are doomed, creatively speaking, from the get-go. It was their considered judgment that the success of the film *Lolita* resulted solely from the gimmick of Peter Sellers playing several roles.

"What we are dealing with," said Kubrick at our first real talk about the situation, "is film by fiat, film by frenzy." What infuriated him most was that the "brains" of the production company could evaluate the entire film—commercially, aesthetically, morally, whatever—in terms of the tour de force performance of one actor. I was amazed that he handled it as well as he did. "I have come to realize," he explained, "that such crass and grotesque stipulations are the *sine qua non* of the motion-picture business." And it was in this spirit that he accepted the studio's condition that this film, as yet untitled, "would star Peter Sellers in at least four major roles."

It was thus understandable that Kubrick should practically freak when a telegram from Peter arrived one morning:

Dear Stanley:
I am so very sorry to tell you that I am having serious difficulty with the various roles. Now hear this: there is no way, repeat, no way, I can play the Texas pilot, 'Major King Kong.' I have a complete block against that accent. Letter from Okin [his agent] follows. Please forgive.

Peter S.

For a few days Kubrick had been in the throes of a Herculean effort to give up cigarettes and had forbidden smoking anywhere in the building. Now he immediately summoned his personal secretary and assistant to bring him a pack pronto.

That evening he persuaded me, since I had been raised in Texas, to make a tape of Kong's dialogue, much of which he had already written (his announcement of the bomb targets and his solemn reading of the Survival Kit Contents, etc.). In the days that followed, as scenes in the plane were written I recorded them on tape so that they would be ready for Sellers, if and when he arrived. Kubrick had been on the phone pleading with him ever since receiving the telegram. When he finally did show up, he had with him the latest state-of-the-art portable tape recorder, specially designed for learning languages. Its ultrasensitive earphones were so oversized they resembled some kind of eccentric hat or space headgear. From the office we would see Sellers pacing between the lilac bushes, script in hand, his face tiny and obscured beneath his earphones. Kubrick found it a disturbing image. "Is he kidding?" he said. "That's exactly the sort of thing that would bring some Brit heat down for weirdness." I laughed, but he wasn't joking. He phoned the production manager, Victor Linden, right away.

"Listen, Victor," I heard him say, "you'd better check out Pete and those earphones. He may be *stressing.* . . . Well, I think he ought to cool it with the earphones. Yeah, it looks like he's trying to ridicule the BBC or something, know what I'm saying? All we need is to get shut down for a crazy stunt like that. Jesus Christ."

Victor Linden was the quintessential thirty-five-year-old English gentleman of the Eton-Oxford persuasion, the sort more likely to join the Foreign Office than the film industry; and, in fact, on more than one occasion I overheard him saying, "With some of us, dear boy, the wogs begin at Calais."

As production manager, it was his job to arrange for, among other things, accommodations for members of the company, including a certain yours truly. "I've found some digs for you," he said, "in Knightsbridge, not far from Stanley's place. I'm afraid they may not be up to Beverly Hills standards, but I think you'll find them quite pleasant.... The main thing, of course, is that you'll be close to Stanley, because of his writing plan."

Stanley's "writing plan" proved to be a dandy. At five A.M., the car would arrive, a large black Bentley, with a back seat the size of a small train compartment—two fold-out desk tops, perfect over-the-left-shoulder lighting, controlled temperature, dark gray windows. In short, an ideal no-exit writing situation. The drive from London to Shepperton took an hour more or less, depending on the traffic and the density of the unfailing fog. During this trip we would write and rewrite, usually the pages to be filmed that day.

It was at a time when the Cold War was at its most intense. As part of the American defense strategy, bombing missions were flown daily toward targets deep inside the Soviet Union, each B-52 carrying a nuclear bomb more powerful than those used on Hiroshima and Nagasaki combined. Bombers were instructed to continue their missions unless they received the recall code at their "fail-safe" points.

In my Knightsbridge rooms, I carefully read *Red Alert*, a book written by an ex-RAF intelligence officer named Peter George that had prompted Stanley's original interest. Perhaps the best thing about the book was the fact that the national security regulations in England, concerning what could and could not be published, were extremely lax by American standards. George had been able to reveal details concerning the "fail-safe" aspect of nuclear deterrence (for example, the so-called black box and the CRM Discriminator)—revelations that, in the spy-crazy U.S.A. of the Cold War era, would have been downright treasonous. Thus the entire complicated technology of nuclear deterrence in *Dr. Strangelove* was based on a bedrock of authenticity that gave the film what must have been its greatest strength: credibility.

The shooting schedule, which had been devised by Victor Linden and of course Kubrick—who scarcely let as much as a trouser pleat go unsupervised—called for the series of scenes that take place inside a B-52 bomber to be filmed first. Peter Sellers had mastered the tricky Texas twang without untoward incident, and then had completed the first day's shooting of Major Kong's lines in admirable fashion. Kubrick was delighted. The following morning, however, we were met at the door by Victor Linden.

"Bad luck," he said, with a touch of grim relish, "Sellers has taken a *fall*. Last night, in front of that Indian restaurant in King's Road. You know the one, Stanley, the posh one you detested. Well, he slipped getting out of the car. Rather nasty I'm afraid. Sprain of ankle, perhaps a hairline fracture." The injury was not as serious as everyone had feared it might be. Sellers arrived at the studio shortly after lunch, and worked beautifully through a couple of scenes. Everything seemed fine until we broke for tea and Kubrick remarked in the most offhand manner, "Ace [the co-pilot] is sitting taller than Peter."

Almost immediately, he announced that we would do a run-through of another scene (much further along in the shooting schedule), which required Major Kong to move from the cockpit to the bomb-bay area via two eight-foot ladders. Sellers negotiated the first, but coming down the second, at about the fourth rung from the bottom, one of his legs abruptly buckled, and he tumbled and sprawled, in obvious pain, on the unforgiving bomb-bay floor.

It was Victor Linden who again brought the bad news, the next day, after Sellers had undergone a physical exam in Harley Street. "The completion-bond people," he announced gravely, "know about Peter's injury and the physical demands of the Major Kong role. They say they'll pull out if he plays the part." Once that grim reality had sunk in, Kubrick's response was an extraordinary tribute to Sellers as an actor: "We can't replace him with another *actor*, we've got to get an authentic character from life, someone whose acting career is secondary—a real-life cowboy." Kubrick, however, had not visited the United States in about fifteen years, and was not familiar with the secondary actors of the day. He asked for my opinion and I immediately suggested big Dan ("Hoss Cartwright") Blocker. He hadn't heard of Blocker, or even—so eccentrically isolated had he become—of the TV show *Bonanza*.

"How *big* a man is he?" Stanley asked.

"Bigger than John Wayne," I said.

We looked up his picture in a copy of *The Players' Guide* and Stanley decided to go with him without further query. He made arrangements for a script to be delivered to Blocker that afternoon, but a cabled response from Blocker's agent arrived in quick order: "Thanks a lot, but the material is too pinko for Dan. Or anyone else we know for that matter. Regards, Leibman, CMA."

As I recall, this was the first hint that this sort of political interpretation of our work-in-progress might exist. Stanley seemed genuinely surprised and disappointed. Linden, however, was quite resilient. "Pinko. . ." he said with a sniff. "Unless I'm quite mistaken, an English talent agency would have used the word 'subversive.'"

Years earlier, while Kubrick was directing the western called *One-Eyed Jacks* (his place was taken by Marlon "Bud" Brando, the producer and star of the film, following an ambiguous contretemps), he'd noticed the authentic qualities of the most natural thesp to come out of the west, an actor with the homey sobriquet of Slim Pickens.

Slim Pickens, born Louis Bert Lindley in Texas in 1919, was an unschooled cowhand who traveled the rodeo circuit from El Paso to Montana, sometimes competing in events, other times performing the dangerous work of rodeo clown—distracting the bulls long enough for injured cowboys to be removed from the arena. At one point, a friend persuaded him to accept work as a stunt rider in westerns. During an open call for *One-Eyed Jacks,* Brando noticed him and cast him in the role of the uncouth deputy sheriff. Except for the occasional stunt work on location, Slim had never been anywhere off the small-town western rodeo circuit, much less outside the U.S. When his agent told him about this remarkable job in England, he asked what he should wear on his trip there. His agent told him to wear whatever he would if he were "going into town to buy a sack of feed"—which meant his Justin boots and wide-brimmed Stetson.

"He's in the office with Victor," Stanley said, "and I don't think they can understand each other. Victor said he arrived in costume. Go and see if he's all right. Ask him if his hotel is okay and all that." When I reached the production office, I saw Victor first, his face furrowed in consternation as he perched in the center of his big Eames wingbat. Then I saw Slim Pickens, who was every inch and ounce the size of the Duke, leaning one elbow to the wall, staring out the window.

"This place," I heard him drawl, "would make one helluva good horse pasture . . . if there's any water."

"Oh, I believe there's water, all right," Victor was absurdly assuring him when he saw me. "Ah, there you are, dear boy," he said. "This is Mr. Slim Pickens. This is Terry Southern." We shook hands, Slim grinning crazily.

"Howdy," he drawled, as gracious as if I were a heroine in an old western. "Mighty proud to know yuh." I went straight to our little makeshift bar, where I had stashed a quart of Wild Turkey specifically for the occasion, which I was ballpark certain would meet his requirements.

"Do you reckon it's too early for a drink, Slim?" I asked. He guffawed, then shook his head and crinkled his nose, as he always did when about to put someone on. "Wal, you know ah think it was jest this mornin' that ah was tryin' to figure out if and when ah ever think it was too early fer a drink, an' damned if ah didn't come up bone dry! Hee-hee-hee!" He cackled his falsetto laugh. "Why hell yes, I'll have a drink with you. Be glad to."

"How about you, Victor?" I asked. His reply was a small explosion of coughs and "hrumphs."

"Actually, it *is* a bit early for me in point of fact," he spluttered. "I've got all those bloody meetings. . . ." I poured a couple and handed one to Slim.

"Stanley wanted me to find out if you got settled in at your hotel, Slim, and if everything is all right." Slim had this unusual habit of sometimes prefacing his reply to a question with a small grimace and a wipe of his mouth against the back of his hand, a gesture of modesty or self-deprecation somehow. "Wal," he said, "it's like this ole friend of mine from Oklahoma says: Jest gimme a pair of loose-fittin' shoes, some tight pussy, and a warm place to shit, an' ah'll be all right."

We were occupying three of the big sound stages at Shepperton: one of them for the War Room set, another for the B-52 bomber set and a third that accommodated two smaller sets, General Ripper's office, including its corridor with Coke machine and telephone booth ("If you try any perversion in there, I'll blow your head off"), and the General Turgidson motel-room set. The B-52 set, where we were shooting at the time, consisted of an actual B-52 bomber, or at least its nose and forward fuselage, suspended about fifteen feet above the floor of the stage. They were between takes when I climbed into the cockpit area where they were doing "character shots": individual close-ups of the co-pilot scrutinizing a *Penthouse* centerfold, the navigator practicing his card tricks, the radar operator wistfully reading a letter from home. Short snippets of action meant to establish the crew as legendary boy-next-door types. Conspicuously absent from the line-up was the bombardier and single black member of the crew, James Earl Jones, or Jimmy, as everyone called him. A classic thespian of high purpose, Jones was about as cultured and scholarly as it is possible for an actor to be, with a voice and presence that were invariably compared to Paul Robeson's.

Kubrick came over to where I was standing, but he remained absorbed in what he called "this obligatory *Our Town* character crap that always seems to come off like a parody of *All Quiet on the Western Front*," a movie that took an outlandish amount of time to focus on the individual behavioral quirks of every man in the regiment. "The only rationale for doing it now," Kubrick said, "is that you're making fun of that historic and corny technique of character delineation." Just as he started to go back to the camera, I saw that his eye was caught by something off the set. "Look at that," he said, "Slim and Jimmy are on a collision course."

Slim was ambling along the apron of the stage toward where Jimmy was sitting by the prop truck absorbed in his script. "Why don't you go down there," Kubrick went on, "and introduce them." It was not so much a question as a very pointed suggestion, perhaps even, it occurred to me, a direct order. I bounded down the scaffolding steps and across the floor of the stage, just in time to intercept Slim in full stride a few feet from where Jimmy was sitting.

"Hold on there, Slim," I said. "I want you to meet another member of the cast." Jimmy got to his feet. "James Earl Jones—Slim Pickens." They shook hands but both continued to look equally puzzled. They had obviously never heard of each other. Somehow

I knew the best route to some kind of rapprochement would be through Jones. "Slim has just finished working on a picture with Marlon Brando," I said.

"Oh well," he boomed, "that must have been very interesting indeed. . . . Yes, I should very much like to hear what it is like to work with the great Mr. Brando."

As if the question were a cue for a well-rehearsed bit of bumpkin business, Slim began to hem and haw, kicking at an imaginary rock on the floor. "Wal," he drawled, his head to one side, "you know ah worked with Bud Brando for right near a full year, an' durin' that time ah never seen him do one thing that wudn't *all man* an' *all white.*"

When I asked Jimmy about it later, he laughed. His laugh, it must be said, is one of the all-time great laughs. "I was beginning to think," and there were tears in his eyes as he said it, "that I must have imagined it."

The quality of Jones's voice comes through most clearly as he delivers the last line of the *Strangelove* script before the bomb is released. The ultimate fail-safe device requires the manual operation of two final safety switches, to insure that the bomb will never be dropped by mistake. Major Kong's command over the intercom is brisk: "Release second safety!" Jones's response, although measured, is unhesitating. He reaches out and moves the lever. It is in his acknowledgement of the order, over the intercom, that he manages to imbue the words with the fatalism and pathos of the ages: "*Second safety . . .*"

Not long afterward, we began shooting the famous eleven-minute "lost pie fight," which was to come near the end of the movie. This footage began at a point in the War Room where the Russian ambassador is seen, for the second time, surreptitiously taking photographs of the Big Board, using six or seven tiny spy-cameras disguised as a wristwatch, a diamond ring, a cigarette lighter, and cufflinks. The head of the Joint Chiefs of Staff, Air Force General Buck Turgidson (George C. Scott) catches him in flagrante and, as before, tackles him and throws him to the floor. They fight furiously until President Merkin Muffley intervenes:

"This is the War Room, gentlemen! How dare you fight in here!"

General Turgidson is unfazed. "We've got the Commie rat red-handed this time, Mr. President!"

The detachment of four military police, which earlier escorted the ambassador to the War Room, stands by as General Turgidson continues: "Mr. President, my experience in these matters of espionage has caused me to be more skeptical than your average Joe. I think these cameras," he indicates the array of ingenious devices, "may be dummy cameras, just to put us off. I say he's got the real McCoy concealed on his person. I would like to have your permission, Mr. President, to have him fully searched."

"All right," the president says, "permission granted."

General Turgidson addresses the military police: "Okay boys, you heard the president. I want you to search the ambassador thoroughly. And due to the tininess of his equipment do not overlook any of the seven bodily orifices." The camera focuses on the face of the ambassador as he listens and mentally calculates the orifices with an expression of great annoyance.

"Why you capitalist swine!" he roars, and reaches out of the frame to the huge three-tiered table that was wheeled in earlier. Then he turns back to General Turgidson, who now has a look of apprehension on his face as he ducks aside, managing to evade a custard pie that the ambassador is throwing at him. President Muffley has been standing directly behind the general, so that when he ducks, the president is hit directly in the face with the pie. He is so overwhelmed by the sheer indignity of being struck with a pie that he simply blacks out. General Turgidson catches him as he collapses.

"Gentlemen," he intones, "The president has been struck down, in the prime of his life and his presidency. I say massive retaliation!" And he picks up another pie and hurls it at the ambassador. It misses and hits instead General Faceman, the Joint Chief representing the Army. Faceman is furious.

"You've gone too far this time, Buck!" he says, throwing a pie himself, which hits Admiral Pooper, the Naval Joint Chief who, of course, also retaliates. A monumental pie fight ensues.

Meanwhile, parallel to the pie-fight sequence, another sequence is occurring. At about the time that the first pie is thrown, Dr. Strangelove raises himself from his wheelchair. Then, looking rather wild-eyed, he shouts, "Mein Führer, I *can valk!*" He takes a triumphant step forward and pitches flat on his face. He immediately tries to regain the wheelchair, snaking his way across the floor, which is so highly polished and slippery that the wheelchair scoots out of reach as soon as Strangelove touches it. We intercut between the pie fight and Strangelove's snakelike movements—reach and scoot, reach and scoot—which suggest a curious, macabre pas de deux. When the chair finally reaches the wall, it shoots sideways across the floor and comes to a stop ten feet away, hopelessly out of reach.

Strangelove, exhausted and dejected, pulls himself up so that he is sitting on the floor, his back against the wall at the far end of the War Room. He stares for a moment at the surreal activity occurring there, the pie fight appearing like a distant, blurry, white blizzard. The camera moves in on Strangelove as he gazes, expressionless now, at the distant fray. Then, unobserved by him, his right hand slowly rises, moves to the inner pocket of his jacket and, with considerable stealth, withdraws a German Luger pistol and moves the barrel toward his right temple. The hand holding the pistol is seized at the last minute by the free hand and both grapple for its control. The hand grasping the wrist prevails and is able to deflect the pistol's aim so that when it goes off with a tremendous roar, it misses the temple.

The explosion reverberates with such volume that the pie fight freezes. A tableau, of white and ghostly aspect: Strangelove stares for a moment before realizing that he has gained the upper hand. "Gentlemen," he calls out to them. "Enough of these childish games. Vee hab vork to do. Azzemble here pleeze!" For a moment, no one moves. Then a solitary figure breaks rank: It is General Turgidson, who walks across the room to the wheelchair and pushes it over to the stricken Strangelove.

"May I help you into your chair, Doctor?" he asks. He begins wheeling Strangelove across the War Room floor, which is now about half a foot deep in custard pie. They move slowly until they reach the president and the Russian ambassador who are sitting crosslegged, facing each other, building a sandcastle.

"What in Sam Hill—" mutters General Turgidson.

"Ach," says Strangelove. "I think their minds have snapped under the strain. Perhaps they will have to be *institutionalized*."

As they near the pie-covered formation of generals and admirals, General Turgidson announces gravely: "Well, boys, it looks like the future of this great land of ours is going to be in the hands of people like Dr. Strangelove here. So let's hear three for the good doctor!" And as he pushes off again, the eerie formation raise their voices in a thin, apparitionlike lamentation: "Hip, hip, hooray, hip, hip, hooray!" followed by Vera Lynn's rendition of "We'll Meet Again." The camera is up and back in a dramatic long shot as General Turgidson moves across the War Room floor in a metaphorical visual marriage of Mad Scientist and United States Military. The End.

This was a truly fantastic sequence. In the first place it was a strictly one-shot affair; there was neither time nor money to reshoot—which would have meant cleaning the hundred or so uniforms and buying a thousand more custard pies. The studio representatives, who were skeptical of the scene all along, had been excruciatingly clear about the matter: "We're talkin' one take. One take and you're outta here, even if you only got shit in the can!"

So it was with considerable trepidation that we screened the results that evening. It must be recalled that each branch of the military service—Army, Navy, Air Force, Marine—receives a separate budget that determines the welfare and the life-style of its top brass. The pie fight, at its most contentious and prolonged, was not between the Russian ambassador and the United States military but between the rival branches of the U.S. military, and it represented a bitter and unrelenting struggle for congressional appropriations. This continuing jealousy between service branches, which causes each one to exaggerate its needs, precludes any chance of reducing our absurdly high defense budget.

The style and mood of the sequence should have reflected these grim circumstances. Kubrick's major goof was his failure to communicate that idea to the sixty or so pie-throwing admirals and generals, so that the prevailing atmosphere, as it came across on the film, might best be described as bacchanalian—with everyone gaily tossing pies, obviously in the highest of spirits. A disaster of, as Kubrick said, "Homeric proportions." Needless to say, the scene was cut.

It was about this time that word began to reach us, reflecting concern as to the nature of the film in production. Was it anti-American? or just anti-military? And the jackpot question, was it, in fact, anti-American to whatever extent it was anti-military? This "buzz along the rialto" was occasionally fleshed out by an actual Nosey Parker type dropping in from New York or Hollywood on behalf of Columbia Pictures. They usually traveled in pairs, presumably on the theory that sleaze is more palatable if spread somewhat thin.

"I feel like Elisha Cook in one of those early Warner films," said Stanley. "You know, when you learn there's a contract out on you, and all you can do is wait for the hit. They're ruthless," he went on, carried away by the film noir image, "absolutely ruthless."

The early visits of those snoopers (with their little high-speed cameras and voice-activated recorders, which they would try to stash on the set and retrieve later) were harbingers of stressful things to come about nine months later, when the first prints of the film were being sporadically screened at the Gulf and Western Building in New York, and word came back to Old Smoke that the Columbia head honchos, Abe Schneider and Mo Rothman, were never in attendance.

I overheard Stanley on the phone to New York. "Listen, Mo," he said, "don't you think you ought to have a look at the film you're making?" Afterward he told me: "Mo says they've been too busy with the new Carl Foreman film—the one with Bing Crosby singing 'White Christmas' while a soldier is being executed. He said, 'It's not so *zany* as yours, Stanley.' Can you believe it? And that isn't the worst. He also said, get this, he said, 'The publicity department is having a hard time getting a handle on how to promote a comedy about the destruction of the planet.'"

It was the first time I had seen Kubrick utterly depressed, and during the ride back to London, he said, "I have the feeling distribution is totally fucked." The next day, however, he was bouncing with optimism and a bold scheme. "I have learned," he said, "that Mo Rothman is a highly serious *golfer*." In a trice he was on the phone to Abercrombie & Fitch, Manhattan's ultraswank sporting-goods emporium. Some fairly elaborate manipulations (plus an untold cash outlay) got him a "surprise gift" presentation of the store's top-of-the-line electric golf cart, to be delivered to the clubhouse of Rothman's Westchester Country Club.

It is a sad anticlimax to report the negative response on Rothman's part. "The son of a bitch refused to accept it!" Stanley exclaimed. "He said it would be 'bad form.'"

It soon became apparent that no one in the company wished to be associated with the film, as if they were pretending that it had somehow spontaneously come into existence. Kubrick was hopping. "It's like they think it was some kind of immaculate fucking conception," he exclaimed with the ultrarighteous indignation of someone caught in an unsuccessful bribery attempt. It was difficult to contain him. "'Bad form!'" he kept shouting, "Can you imagine *Mo Rothman* saying that? His secretary must have taught him that phrase!"

In the months that followed, the studio continued to distance itself from the film. Even when *Strangelove* received the infrequent good review, it dismissed the critic as a pinko nutcase and on at least one occasion the Columbia Pictures publicity department *defended* the company against the film by saying it was definitely not "anti-U.S. military," but "just a zany novelty flick which did not reflect the views of the corporation in any way." This party line persisted, I believe, until about five years ago, when the Library of Congress announced that the film had been selected as one of the fifty greatest American films of all time—in a ceremony at which I noted Rothman in prominent attendance. Who said satire was "something that closed Wednesday in Philadelphia"?

The Un-American Women

One, they're spooking, two, they're opening letters,
three, there's a body at the bottom of the pool
labeled "Comrade X," and you've been asked to
speak up truthfully or not at all It's like Einstein
lolling on the lawn—somebody *gave* him the telescope,
he wouldn't "buy" one—and our investigator has him
trapped in the viewfinder. Albert! Tell us everything!
We won't blame you for the atom bomb! After all,
you're dead! Four, cancel the code and burn the cipher.
It's no laughing matter when the shit hits the fan—
why are you grinning like that? Are you now
or have you ever been a woman? That's a tricky one,
I know you'd like a stiff rum and coke and ten minutes
alone on the patio to think it over, but
the G-men in the back room are getting anxious;
the Mickey Finn's invented, the hand that
feeds you's quicker than the eye, and in a wink
the powder's in the drink! Our Leader's dozing
in a tank and in his memory we labor mightily.
Are you a German Jew? We sympathize; do you?
The Memory Bank is sad tonight, it's asking
for your friends, they have a future there.
Let's share a pentothal and take a ride;
the garden's full of Government employees
but I'll hold your hand. You make a movie,
I'll write the dialogue: One, we're laughing,
two, we're breaking rules—I'm finished, you're
dead, and as the cipher smolders on the lawn
a cold glow rises from the bottom of the tank:
our Leader starts to speak, and so will you.

The Duck Abandons Hollywood

I flew my long uphill glide to immortality
solo, on flammable acetate. O idle frenzy,
stockpiling cans of cartoons—and what splashy
comeback glitters next week? *Fat chance!*—
this taunt from a gaggle of my dusky betters
dabbling around the lagoon—better? because
more "natural"! My siblings babbling scuttlebutt—
me, guilty? of what betrayal? Human gestures
dignify my tribe, those phantoms in the chalky beam
heal while they gyp and flimflam. Past tense!
yes, radical as any Method stratagem, my hackery
deified suburban angst, bum gigs, tantrums.
Steering thus through fits and suffering,
I grew complex—a troubadour could not but be
bisexual, I reckon, in such a wiggle rig. *Vain
fakery,* stars mutter, swapping their knacks
back and forth amidst the smoke and buzz in Lindy's.
I'm still chipper—no, those soul-sisters flapped
and cackled in my bad dream; they damned me, then
gulped their bubbly gush, and giggled—puzzling mirth . . .

I'm a chronic dope, sure thing, fondling this enigmatic image—oh, whacked out in my den I drivel, in spent or flaky vein. Up there my horrid flocks disrobe upon that indifferent retina which is the paradise of quarantine— what's each verbal mouthful worth, what are dreams patched up from— watercolors in a box? And when I tally up what booty this greed for god- hood got me—*numbers flicker; blank screen*—my feathered bulk chokes on misery, and nods off with the spirits—mayhap in our 3-D Cincrama Hunting- Ground we'll reminisce and chortle—crystal spirits in a jug of hooch.

Playland–
Setting the Scene

I

First things first.

She was born Melba Mae Toolate (or maybe not, but certainly, or so I think, close enough, although Myrna Marie Toolate still has its adherents, the way Los Angeles with a hard "g" also has its core vote) in San Bernardino, California, April 28, 1928. That is, if she was not born in Yuma, Arizona, on the same date a year earlier (in other words, April 28, 1927), or then again in Shoshone, California, October 29, 1929, but that was the day the stock market crashed, and a few years later, after Melba Mae Toolate became Baby Blue Tyler, Hollywood's number-one cinemoppet and biggest box-office star, studio publicists, always looking for an item, would claim that her birth was America's only bright spot that day, which did not exactly lend the date, as Blue Tyler's birthday, verisimilitude.

Her father died shortly before her birth, or shortly thereafter, or perhaps he was in prison in Ohio when she was born, or then again maybe it was in Pennsylvania, Nebraska, or Montana. The prison stories surfaced only after her disgrace; Blue Tyler was a woman, a child really, to whom disgrace attached itself with a certain regularity, but the disgrace here in question was her appearance before the House Committee on Un-American Activities, when she was either nineteen, twenty, or twenty-one years old. The prison reports came up again after her disappearance from what *Collier's* magazine called "the baleful glare of the public eye," in any event when those same studio publicists who had been so quick to claim, for Jimmy Fidler's deadline, that Blue Tyler was born the day the market went belly up were no longer available to keep the legend, such as it was (and even more so such as it became), free from taint.

Anyway. Melba's father (if indeed he was). Among other names, he was known as Herman Toolate or Herbert Tulahti ("too-late" and "too-lah-tee" being the two conflicting pronunciations of the name she abandoned when she became, or was reborn as, Blue Tyler), or (this from those French cinéastes who kept Blue Tyler's torch from being extinguished in those decades when she was, as it were, in the desert) Henri Tulaté. Mr. Toolate (or if you will Mr. Tulahti or M. Tulaté) was in some accounts a pharmacist, in others a would-be trombonist or a failed Tin Pan Alley songwriter (sample unpublished song titles: "Mimi from Miami" and "Yolanda from Yuma," the latter giving sustenance to those who favored Arizona as Melba Mae's birthplace, and the added possibility that Yolanda was in fact her real name, a father's hymn to his daughter), or even a ballroom dancer who had murdered his partner during a dance marathon in 1931 (this scenario, in a French monograph on Blue Tyler's career, stolen without apology from Horace McCoy's *They Shoot Horses, Don't They?*).

The former Melba Mae Toolate's musical talent, such as it was, was said to come from this man cast as her father (in his trombonist, songwriter, or marathon-dancer incarnations), unless it came via her mother (Irma in most cases, although Erna, Ursula, and heaven knows how many other Christian names were also candidates), a God-fearing (in later revisionist versions, as theological fashions changed and theories about the death of God were abroad in the land, God-hating) woman who taught piano, or the harp, or (this from a piece in *Film Comment* entitled "The Geometry of Dance in the Classic Hollywood Musicals") mathematics. Irma (or Erna or Ursula) Toolate's emergence as the more dominant influence on Melba Mae was a feminist theory that came into currency after the brief reappearance of Blue Tyler as a middle-aged woman in Hamtramck, Michigan, when for a moment she became, to her surprise (although I cannot say amusement, because when one spends an entire professional life cosseted by the apparatus of a motion-picture studio, one does not easily learn to be amused at one's own expense), a heroine of the women's movement, a victim, in that liturgy, of the system and the male oppressors who would extinguish any spark of female spirit or independence.

You begin to see the difficulty.

II

Chuckie O'Hara died yesterday. The obituary in the *Times* said he was seventy-seven, but I knew he was older than that, to the very end vain about his age in that poofter way of his, eighty-two or eighty-three more likely, because when he lost his leg on Peleliu he had already received an Oscar nomination, for directing *Lily of the Valley*. Most of the obits carried the picture, the famous photograph, of Chuckie testifying before the Un-American Activities Committee, the day he took off his wooden leg when the chairman asked if he was now or ever had been a Communist. It was quite a sight on those grainy old Movietone newsreels I tracked down and ran when I was trying to find out anything at all about Blue Tyler, who as it happened was the star of *Lily of the Valley*, her performance earning her a third Academy nomination, all before she was twelve.

In the stock footage, Chuckie began pulling up his pant leg just as he started to answer the chairman's question. Every eye in the hearing room was on him as he unbuckled that old-fashioned prosthetic device with all the straps, laid it on the witness table, and then said, clear as a bell, "Yes, Mr. Chairman, I was a Communist," not taking the First, as the Ten had done, and not the Fifth either, and he listed the dates, from October 1938 to July 1941, and no, he would respectfully decline to name names, all the time massaging that raw stump of the leg he lost on Orange Beach. It was a real director's touch, a perfect piece of business. Chuckie always knew exactly how to stage a scene, and he knew that no one at the hearing was listening to what he had to say, they were just looking at that stump, all pulpy and white with red cross-hatching where the stitches had been. "Darling," he told me when I asked him about that day in front of the committee, "it was divine." Sydney Allen stole the hearing scene and used it in one of his pictures when it was safe to do safe pictures about the blacklist. The *Times* tried to get a quote from Sydney for Chuckie's obit, but Mr. Allen's spokesman said that Mr. Allen was in the cutting room and was not available for comment. Sydney never disappoints, as always a thoroughbred shitheel.

In a movie, Chuckie's performance would have taken the steam out of the hearings, which naturally it did in Sydney Allen's piece of crap, but in real life, of course, it didn't. Only time accomplished that. Still the scene had good value. Chuckie was certainly a Red, he admitted that, but I doubt if it had anything to do with politics. Blue told me it was because he was really stuck on Reilly Holt, the writer at Paramount, and a high-muckety-muck in the Party, and from things Chuckie told me later I suspect she was getting close to the truth. In his defense, it should also be said that no one on that committee had ever hit a beach, let alone had a leg blown off on one.

The Marine Corps must have had some idea about Chuckie's politics, it had to be why he was never given a commission, when they were making ADs from Poverty Row captains and majors. Chuckie said he preferred being an enlisted man anyway. The farm boys in the barracks were more susceptible to my roguish charms than officers in a BOQ might have been, he said, the roughest of rough trade, my dear, it comes from being so louche with all those sheep on cold winter nights. And the farm boys were more than compensation enough for having to salute Jack Ford and Willie Wyler, even, sweet mother of God, DZ.

But if the Corps did not think Chuckie was officer material, it did realize that Corporal, later Sergeant, Charlton O'Hara, USMCR, was a pretty country-fair director, just the man to shoot invasions, and so they gave him a film crew and put him on the beach with the first wave when the Fifth Marines hit Cape Gloucester the day after Christmas 1943 ("Not the way one would ordinarily choose to spend Boxing Day, dear," he said once), and then again nine months later with the first wave at Peleliu, a pointless and bloody fiasco, again with the Fifth Marines. All the marine brass really wanted was film of jarheads hitting the beach to show Congress when it was time for the next year's appropriations. To the Corps, Chuckie's politics (and the sexual orientation the brass must have suspected) did not matter as much as the footage he was getting, when the chances were he was going to end up in a body bag anyway, a dead Commie nance, longevity not generally accruing to people who landed often enough with the first wave. Meaning Chuckie was probably lucky only to lose his right leg from the knee down on D-Plus Two at Peleliu, Orange Beach, from an unexploded mortar round buried in the sand that he accidentally kicked while he was moving his crew around the beach looking for a better angle. Force of habit, the old Cosmopolitan Pictures training, directors at Cosmo always overcovered so that any mistakes could be fixed in the editing room.

Chuckie was blacklisted after he testified, no studio would hire him, no independent would back his projects. He could have gone to England but he hated the cold and he hated the dark wet English winters. Anyway the blacklist was not as much of an economic hardship for Chuckie as it was for so many others in the same boat because he was rich; his family owned most of the highway billboards in the state of California. Not old money, darling, he told me, but money, and pots of it. He left his tiny perfect house in the Hollywood Hills and moved up to his family's place in the Carmel Highlands, where he was in no danger of being constantly reminded of the Industry from which he had been banished. The old O'Hara house on the Carmel bluffs looked as if it grew out of the rock formations that fell into the Pacific hundreds of feet below, and there on the sea he spent his period of exile with his trick of the moment and with his dotty old mother, Vera O'Hara, who even when I met Chuckie several decades later was always asking him when he was going to get married. That was when I was taping his memories of Blue Tyler, and he was at the same time pumping me about her. During the hours and days we spent together, I kept trying to imagine his life in those years when he was a professional nonperson. All over the Carmel house, there were photographs of Chuckie from that period; as much as any of the actors he directed, Chuckie loved having his picture taken, and in fact favored catamites who were photographers, although he never photographed them in turn. In the comfort of this Elba, he seemed to want for nothing, the man of principle as the man of leisure.

So I can understand the surprise of those who had canonized him when one day Chuckie flew to Washington on his own and in executive session with the committee's investigator purged himself. Because of his earlier appearance—a public-relations disaster the committee did not wish to repeat—he was treated with kid gloves, and his testimony was never made public. There was only an announcement that he had appeared voluntarily and that his testimony would be most helpful in allowing the committee to prepare its final report. That was it. Chuckie never said who he had named—less than I could have, more than I should have, was all he would tell me—and he went back to work as untroubled by his decision as he was by most of the events in his life. Why did you do it? I asked. Not very complicated, he answered. What it boiled down to was that he missed working. He missed the costume tests and the looping and the mixing sessions and the big mugs of coffee the script girl would hand him during the shoot and the crossword puzzles he would work with his thick black Mont Blanc pen while the DP was lighting the next scene. I could never feature myself as this queen hero of the revolution, he said during one of our tapings, it was in the most revolting taste.

For a while after his recantation, he worked steadily if without particular distinction, accepted again in the commissaries and the private studio dining rooms, at the same time denounced as a pariah and stool pigeon by those of his peers who had been so quick to acclaim him a hero on that earlier occasion before the committee when he had removed his prosthetic leg. The younger historians of this period, ideologically correct, dismiss him as absent character and kidney, but they were never able to appreciate the social weave of Hollywood, what it was like to live and work there, to understand that the priority was always making pictures, the black sheep accepted back in the fold always a reliable story line. After a time, he more or less slipped into professional oblivion, doing an occasional Hallmark Hall of Fame special, but never segment television, Chuckie was too much a snob for that, he had after all directed Crawford and Davis and Kate and Claudette and Blue Tyler.

Ah, yes. Blue Tyler. Or Melba Mae Toolate, as she had become once again when I sought her out in Hamtramck, Michigan, her real name the perfect disguise. Chuckie knew so many of Blue's early secrets, as I knew so many of her later ones, although she was such an elaborate fantast (a fastidious construct, liar being more to the point) that no one could ever really pin down the truth, such as it was, about her. Melba Mae covered her tracks.

Chuckie's stories were wonderful. Not always believable, but wonderful. He tended to look at life as if he was setting up a shot, his hands joined at the thumbs, framing what he wanted the camera to see. A story was only meant to advance the action, and sooner than I should have I found myself going along with him, adding some set decoration of my own. You get in the mood. See the possibilities. Did it really matter if what happened did not actually happen that way? Who was to know? Everything is subjective.

We were just advancing the action. Story conferencing the truth. A shading here, a shading there, in the interest, always we would tell ourselves, of clarification. Facts are unforgiving, so fuck facts, make the scenes work.

Anyway, Chuckie's stories, such as they were. About Blue, of course. And her passion for Jacob King. People in Hollywood have always had this romantic idea about gangsters, and Jacob with his slick hair and perfect teeth and his dark brooding looks and his volcanic furies satisfied every fantasy. Even his sexual appendage was given demonic proportions, the *schlong* on him, the *schwanss*, the *schmekelah*, Chuckie said, and he a student of such instruments, with a student's capacity for priapic exaggeration, a foot and a half, I saw it in the shower at Hillcrest. The venue explained Chuckie's lapse into Yiddish, the anti-Semitism that came so easily to him no reason not to play gin at the Industry's top Jewish country club, to take a little steam and case a few cocks in the locker room. This blissful reverie of an aged pederast allowed me to contemplate how many psychic miles Jacob King had traveled from the Red Hook section of Brooklyn where he was born to the shower room at Hillcrest where Chuckie could swoon over his swinging dick. And Jacob the only man in that shower of whom it could be claimed that he had made his bones at the age of twelve. Or was it ten? Or had he just been brought along as a decoy, on that hit when he was ten, because his youth made the professional cannons doing the dirty less suspicious looking?

Jacob King admitted nothing.

And denied nothing.

Twenty or thirty times he had whacked someone out.

Or so people said.

Did I know, Chuckie said, that Jake once killed somebody by wrapping his face in duct tape so he couldn't breathe? A murder meant to make a statement.

Or so the story was.

Chuckie saw the duct tape caper as a high-angle crane shot, with a slow pan down, then a 120 frame hold on the mummified victim before the cut.

When Jacob King was killed, his left eye was blown out of its socket and landed on the unfinished portrait he was having painted of himself. Like a piece of snot, Chuckie said about the eyeball. Jacob was wearing jodhpurs in the portrait and laced boots and a beige silk shirt and a polka-dot ascot. Yet another indication of the mileage from Red Hook he had put on his psychic pedometer.

Or perhaps he was only traveling in place. On a treadmill with a fancier wardrobe.

It was said that Blue bought the portrait after Jacob King was killed. In any event, no one ever saw it again.

Chuckie said that Jacob always carried a silver Tiffany locket in which he kept two of Blue's pubic hairs. Why just two? I said. Why not one? Or one short and curly for every time he fucked her? They couldn't have taken up all that much room if the locket was big enough. It wasn't like it was a load of hay.

These were the sort of questions I always asked. Chuckie would never answer, but would just go off on another tangent about someone else. About Blue's lawyer, Lilo Kusack, and Lilo's girlfriend, Rita Lewis. About J. F. French. The Mogul. Founder of Cosmopolitan Pictures. J. F. French claimed to have personally discovered Blue Tyler when she was only four years old. Arthur French figured in Chuckie's reminiscences, too. Arthur was J. F.'s son and Blue's designated fiancé when she was under contract to Cosmopolitan. Chuckie saw the whole story as a movie, when his mind stopped wandering. It will be my comeback picture, he said. And then he would say, doesn't it bother you the way these vile children directors say *film*? We made *pictures*. Adding after a moment, "I sound like some faggot female impersonator doing Norma Desmond."

I was surprised at how many people turned out for Chuckie's funeral. All the oldtimers who were still around, and for whom a funeral was an outing, many of them with canes and walkers and private nurses. In the end he was one of them, whatever his transgressions; membership in the closed society of the motion-picture industry is almost never revoked for moral failings.

Of course Chuckie had scripted the service, down to the music cues. He wanted a bugler to blow the Marine Corps hymn at his graveside, slow tempo, "From the halls of Montezuma, To the shores of Tripoli," and then a segue into taps. Even from beyond the grave the *fageleh* son of a bitch was manipulating me.

And I cried, as I knew I was meant to.

The Desert in Bloom

(from *Byways*)

Why can't you remember the Nevada
Desert awash with bright-colored
Flowers when we camped not far
From Tonapah that April long ago?
It was soon after we had met in
San Francisco and fallen in love.
You were George's sister, the
Beautiful Poet's beautiful sister,
That's how I got to know you.
Surely you must remember how the
Desert that was so harsh all the
Rest of the year, rocks and gray
Sand, had suddenly burst into
Bloom, a salute to Persephone in
Almost violent praise of spring,
A salute that would last only a
Few weeks till the snow moisture
In the ground would be exhausted.
Rexroth had loaned us a tent and
We gathered dry cactus to cook
Over an open fire. At night we
Heard the soft cooing of doves
From all around us in the dark
But at dawn they ceased their
Complaining. You said that they
Reminded you of the doves in
Provence when you were there

As a girl, the *roucoulement des*
Colombes that the troubadours
And their ladies had heard in
The castle gardens, recording
Their sound in their *cansos.*
The ground was hard under our
Sleeping bags, the desert gets
Chilly at night, so cold that
Sometimes we had to squeeze
Into one bag, skin to skin,
Enlaced together. At night in the
Desert the stars seem twice as
Bright as anywhere else; when
We lay on our backs we would
Look up into the vastness, trying
To locate the constellations
And remember the names that were
Given them by the Greeks in the
Myths how many thousands of years
Ago. Andromeda and the Dioscuri;
Cassiopeia, whom Perseus saved
From the sea monster; Orion, the
Mighty hunter; the Pleiades, whose
Comings and goings tell the seasons;
Berenike, whose pretty lock of
Hair has lived in song; the lion,
The dragon, and the swan. Your
People were Jewish but your
Beauty was more of Attica than
Of Phoenicia, great brown eyes,
Dark hair and olive skin. The
Girls of Lesbos would have adored

You but you were not of their
Kind. Your body is described
In the *Song of Songs;* not a
Fraction of an inch would I
Have changed in its proportions
If I were a sculptor. The desert
Was empty and I would ask you
To lie naked in the sun, now
And then changing your pose, a
Moving sculpture. You had the
Marks of Eros, a girl fit for
The Mysteries. Liquid as the
Fountain Arethusa. And you were
Funny and endearing and passionate.
Holding hands, we took walks on
The endless desert before the sun
Became too hot. I picked flowers
And made a multicolored garland
For your hair. The handmaiden
Of Aphrodite, *venerandam.* In the
Shade of the tent I read you the
Exquisite love sonnets of Louise
Labé, which aroused us to make
Love again, hot as it was, the
Sweat glistening on our bodies.
One day we drove into Tonapah,
Now the slumbering ruin of the
Old hell-&-damnation mining
Town, where once fortunes of
Gold were won and lost at the
Tables, and men killed for it.
The streets were empty, but in

What is left of the grand Hotel
California we found an old man
Dozing on top of the green
Gaming table; we woke him up
And shot craps with silver dollars
For chips. We stayed on the desert
For three days, when we had used
Up the water we had brought
With us in cans.

Now after fifty years we're in
Touch again. You've had four
Husbands and I'm on my third
Marriage. You say that you
Can hardly remember our love-
Making on the flowering desert.
How can that be? For me it's
As fresh as if it only happened
Yesterday. I see you clear with
My garland in your hair. Now we
Are two old people nursing our
Aches. What harm can there be
In remembering? We cannot hurt
One another now.

The Women

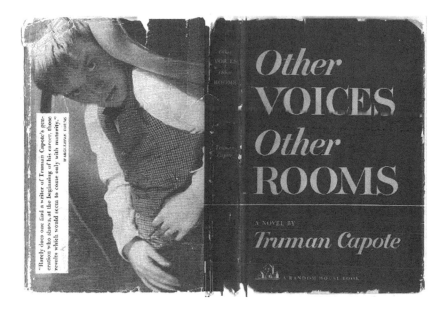

Truman Capote became a woman in 1947, the year this photograph was taken. Much has been made of it since its appearance on the dust jacket of Capote's first novel, *Other Voices, Other Rooms.*

Actually, it is not a photograph, but a shadow ground through publicity, coming out the other side as something else. The mind cannot be blank in the face of it. It is an image that is an assertion, a point, asserting this: I am a woman.

In 1947, women did not publish books. So determined to be authors were they—Jean Stafford, Carson McCullers, Marguerite Young, say—that they buttoned themselves up on dust jackets in the image of the male American author (generally Hemingway). Truman Capote became a woman in 1947 just when "real" women would not or could not. And the woman he became in this photograph (itself better written than *Other Voices, Other Rooms*) wanted to be fucked by you and by any idea of femininity that had fucked you up.

In his writing, Capote addressed this issue only once—in the "factual" short story "Dazzle," which appeared in his last collection of writings, *Music for Chameleons*. The story is sentimental because Capote could never write of himself—of what he wanted rather than what he imagined for others—without being sentimental. Another form of lying. In "Dazzle" he wrote, "I had a secret, something that was bothering me, something that was really worrying me very much. . . . 'I don't want to be a boy. I want to be a girl.'"

By becoming the most famous woman author—not writer, an important distinction—of his generation, Truman Capote prevented other women authors from being popular, admired, celebrated. For a time. He was the model of potential for women who wrote and an image of what they might become if they continued to write: popular, admired, celebrated.

The photograph, which also shows Capote as an American woman author of style (the vest as opposed to a jacket, his translucent, flat fingernails, the watered or greased hair flattening the top of his head with the light hitting it just so, his eyebrows plucked or raised in mild astonishment, something to be fucked somehow) was too much for one or two of his peers who did not have the will to deconstruct their bodies as language.

Capote's career as a woman author makes a more interesting narrative than *Other Voices, Other Rooms*. And his generally male writer friends realized that what separated them from Truman Capote was his will to create a self that existed apart from writing and, hence, his ability to become an image accessible to publicity. Donald Windham's peevish response to this: "The publishing world is what I was aware of Capote's being in. We were both writers. Still, although I was twenty-seven and he was only twenty-three, he was in the publishing world and I was not."

We were both writers. A sentence that beats against Capote's concept of what the author's body means in the world: how it becomes a narrative for other writers to write about. Windham again: "His defense in person was never camouflage; it was always boldness. Once, on a New York street, when he was telling me an anecdote in a high voice accompanied by expansive gestures and saw a burly truck driver glowering at him, he sassed, 'What are you looking at? I wouldn't kiss you for a dollar.'"

Truman Capote lied about this photograph in which he appears to be a woman. He lied about the photograph's intent, claiming in some instances that it had been sent to his publishers upon request by a friend while he was away, or that he was unaware of what he projected in the image. This was the first instance of the disjunction between Capote's image of himself and the meaning he projected to others in images of himself. It was also the first instance of Capote not accepting responsibility for his effect as he effected it, a trope he would repeat within subsequent identities.

Perhaps he was aware of this, of the potential for manipulation of image within the writing and publishing worlds: "This subject [publishing] fascinates me, and I know so much about it I could talk for seven hours. Nonstop. About how publishers work and why you should do this and why you should do that."

As he produced less and less (from 1966 until his death in 1984), women began to be packaged as such and, as such, they became the publishing world's new custodians of "other" language. (Elizabeth Hardwick "confirms her stature . . . [and] has as much to say about women in the world as . . . women on the page," reads part of the jacket copy of her book, *Seduction and Betrayal* [1974].) Capote was left no other recourse than to become a man.

He became a man with the publication of his "big" book, *In Cold Blood* (1966), a book about one man, Perry Smith, a murderer consumed by vanity like the woman Capote believed, upon the book's publication, that he had been. Which is to say that *In Cold Blood* set out to prove, in part, that Truman Capote was no longer a lyrical authoress (of *Other Voices, Other Rooms*, he explained: "What [I] had done has the enigmatic shine of a strangely colored prism held to the light—that and a certain anguished, pleading intensity like the message of a shipwrecked sailor stuffed into a bottle and thrown into the sea"), but a writer validated by his experience in the world of fact (*In Cold Blood: A factual account of multiple murders and their consequences*) and by a largely male literary tradition.

In Cold Blood was a deliberate defense against men, or one man, Norman Mailer, who had called Capote, in the '50s, "as tart as a grand aunt." This statement, a caricature and a diminishment of Capote's role as a powerful woman author, marked how Capote's self-perception, and hence the public perception of him, would have to change. While grand aunts can be powerful, they are not generally perceived as such in the world of publishing. And as women writers eventually became what publishers could sell, albeit with reservations and marginally, Capote could probably advise them the most clearly as to why they "should do this and why [they] should do that." (As he eventually did with the publisher of the *Washington Post*, Katharine Graham—in whose honor he threw his famous Black and White ball—and, to a greater degree, with Barbara "Babe" Paley—"She was the most important person in my life and I the most important in hers"—a woman made powerful through her association with her husband, media chief and CBS chairman William S. Paley.

The image (or reality) of the maiden aunt is one which male power revolts against or finds revolting, in relation to which masculinity defines itself. Capote was not a maiden aunt in the presence of male power; he was, however, a fashionable person in his ambivalence and fear of it. He himself expressed this in a letter to John Malcolm Brinnin: "Maybe I ought to . . . get drunk and play Prometheus like Norman." Which is to say that Truman Capote the woman realized that Truman Capote the man would eventually have to adhere to the publishing world's perception of the male writer if he were to occupy a place in it and be of continued interest to the press.

Capote identified this apparatus—the cultural press, media power—as male and Jewish. "The truth of the matter about it is, the entire cultural press, publishing, . . . criticism . . . television . . . is almost ninety percent Jewish-oriented. I mean, I can't even count on one hand five people of any importance—of real importance— in the media who aren't Jewish." Two Jews at whom he leveled his sentimental anti-Semitism were Norman Mailer and William S. Paley, men who, by all accounts, did not want to be fucked by any idea of femininity that had fucked them up but to fuck their idea of femininity. The determination that Mailer and Paley demonstrated, their absorption in and accumulation of power, was in part to dispel the stereotypical image of the Jewish male, described again and again by Philip Roth and Bernard Malamud—that of a man paralyzed by reflection, powerless to function, voiceless, trying to function separately from the matriarch. Or, in the case of

Paley and Mailer, separately from the one thing that elicited from their women something as potentially powerful as sex: language.

Those powerful Jewish men and their sexual selves were removed enough from Capote's sexuality (whatever that was) to be sexual for him. In *Answered Prayers*, his unfinished novel, the character widely believed to be based on Paley, Sidney Dillon, "conglomateur, adviser to Presidents," is described by Capote's fictitious alter ego, P. B. Jones (who has seen him in a Polaroid belonging to a woman friend), as "a wiry well-constructed man with a hairy chest and a twinkle-grinning tough-Jew face; his bathing trunks . . . rolled to his knees, one hand rested sexily on a hip, and with the other he was pumping a dark fat mouth-watering dick."

That dick—as strong a symbol as any—stretched across Truman Capote's consciousness less because he identified it as being attached to power than because he saw it as an object of desire for women, imagined by some women to be the source of their power. In *Answered Prayers*, the act of romantic love is always recounted in spoken language, not described directly. P. B. Jones's introduction to the formidable woman author Alice Lee Langman, whom he sleeps with and whose protégé he subsequently becomes, is followed by: "Miss Langman was often, in interviews, described as a witty conversationalist; how can a woman be witty when she hasn't a sense of humor?—and she had none, which was her central flaw as a person and as an artist. But she was indeed a talker, a relentless bedroom back-seat driver: . . . 'That's better better and better Billy let me have billy now that's uh uh uh it that's *it* only slower slower and slower now hard hard hit it hard ay ay *los cojones* let me hear them ring now slower slower dradraaaaagdrag it out now hit hard hard ay ay daddy Jesus have mercy Jesus Jesus goddamdaddyamighty come with me Billy come! Come!'"

Capote wrote: "Norman Mailer described [*In Cold Blood*] as a 'failure of the imagination'. . . . Norman Mailer, who has made a lot of money and won a lot of prizes writing nonfiction novels, . . . although he has always been careful never to describe them as 'nonfiction novels.' No matter, he is a good writer and a fine fellow and I'm grateful to have been of some small service to him."

The operative words here are "small" and "service"—"small"

Truman "servicing" Norman on the altar of his art—the creation of the phrase, if not the genre, "nonfiction novel." Even as he published *In Cold Blood,* Capote lost any claim to male authorship by presuming that his factual account of a multiple murder would create him too—in Mailer's image. It is hard to garner privilege when you begin with none—for those who have to reach for it, it remains perpetually out of reach. Mailer would always have it and Capote would not, because Mailer assumed that he did and Capote assumed that he did not.

For several years before 1947 Capote had been a man (a state defined by uninflected ambition) in his pursuit of authorship and his appropriation of the style, syntax, and voice of women authors generally perceived as maiden aunts (Eudora Welty) or maiden-aunts-in-code (lesbian Carson McCullers)—women with careers less powerful than Capote's would eventually be, but powerful in this: before Truman Capote became Truman Capote, they were themselves. Capote was not himself as a writer until *Answered Prayers,* a novel that grew out of his isolation and self-realization, a novel that remained unfinished.

As an ultimately fashionable author, which is to say a person who wrote but also felt uncomfortable with the responsibility of being only a writer, he rode the wave of fashion too, observing power and trends as established by others, change as established by others. Capote was a distinctly American author, one who spoke, read, thought in no other language than American and was, therefore, parochial in his knowledge. He could respond intellectually only to those things he responded to emotionally. There was no other referent for thought. What he responded to before 1947 and thereafter, in a different way, was himself (a man) in relationship to women. Since he spoke no other language than his own ("My voice has been described as high and childish *among other things*"), he had to learn to become an American writer by appropriating the language of other American writers, and what he most responded to intellectually was written by women authors. But his reverence for them was always tempered. (On Flannery O'Connor: "She has some fine moments, that girl." On Carson McCullers: "She was a devil, but I respected her.") He strove to be the ultimate version of them, that, as women, they would never be.

This was also true of Capote becoming a man. He could not simply admire William S. Paley, he had to surpass him in Babe Paley's affection. He had to become a more powerful media figure by becoming recognizably famous. What Truman Capote could not do was reorder Babe Paley's ideas of her own femininity. He only did women on the page. And instead of attempting to reveal their secrets as women, he competed for an understanding of their identity as such. This was the only form of exchange he had with them, and it was different than the other exchanges these women had (or the only other exchanges Capote acknowledged them as having): being with "real" men who fucked them.

Capote's resentment of what these women did without him was based, as was his education as a writer, on an emotional response to two things: the ultimate impossibility of knowing or understanding women's sexual movements (up and down, in, out, around, what, when: the gossip's grid of information versus the writer's nongrid of reflection), and the heterosexual male's desire for them. Capote could not forgive his writing for obfuscating this interest. "My effects prior to *Answered Prayers* seemed overdone," he complained. The writing before *Answered Prayers* lied by taking the (public) fag's easy way out. The writing before *Answered Prayers* was "beautiful," "evocative," "poetic." It was filtered through a skein of perplexity about male and female relations.

Truman Capote could not have become a woman without women authors and editors being interested in him. (Let us leave aside early biographical data for now—how he was abandoned by his alcoholic mother, how he was taken in by maiden aunts and cousins, etc. These facts, while interesting, have more to do with his *process* of self-creation than with the moment he created himself as Truman Capote, the writer and the photograph.)

The women Capote interested and those in whom he was interested were women who were interested in language. Perhaps he saw women as a form of language. Certainly those he was interested in before he became one himself had faces like words. "Not plain, not pretty, arresting rather, with an expression deliberately haunted rather than haunting," Capote wrote of portraits of two women authors published in Richard Avedon's *Observations* in 1957, a sentence interesting in its insistence on definition, in its use of the word "deliberately." Perhaps, even as he used a language of separation to describe them, Capote resented the women's separation from him.

One of the first to be interested in Capote was Rita Smith, a fiction editor at *Mademoiselle*, who published "Miriam," the story, ostensibly, of a girl who can't grow up because she exists only in the mind of an old woman who has not. This story can be read as a sign of Capote's knowledge that he would become a woman, the floor plan, in a sense, of the image Truman Capote would eventually project:

> [Miriam] was thin and fragilely constructed. There was a simple, special elegance in the way she stood. . . . Mrs. Miller decided the truly distinctive feature was not her hair, but her eyes; they were hazel, steady, lacking any childlike quality whatsoever.

Miriam" was the story which garnered Truman Capote—then twenty years old—a great deal of public attention, attracting Bennett Cerf, publisher of Random House, who signed Capote on for his first novel (which became *Other Voices, Other Rooms*).

It was Rita Smith who introduced Capote to her famous sibling, Carson McCullers. McCullers's biographer states, "Never before had Carson been so enthusiastic about promoting another young writer . . . who many people thought served as a model for her final concept of John Henry West," a character in her novel *The Member of the Wedding*. In writing about Capote, Rita Smith all but disappears after his ascension to friendship with McCullers. In order to become a woman more famous than McCullers, Capote needed to build himself on her model and then destroy that model to prevent any subsequent excavation of the genesis of Truman Capote.

While McCullers remained steeped in regionalism (the American South, of which Capote too was a native), Capote went on to become a woman of the world, or enough of one to describe McCullers, once more famous than he, rather condescendingly as "not plain, not pretty, arresting rather"—words that also describe the exact effect of McCullers's writing on Capote, whom McCullers eventually suspected of having "poached on my literary preserves."

Once certain women became interested in Capote, he could begin to understand how to take from their work. What he stole was more syntax than complete style. Take, for instance, the tone of Eudora Welty's "Why I Live at the P.O." (a story written during her literary apprenticeship to another woman author, Katherine Anne Porter):

> I was getting along fine with Mama, Papa-Daddy and Uncle Rondo until my sister Stella-Rondo just separated from her husband and came back home again. . . . Came home from one of those towns up in Illinois and to our complete surprise brought this child of two.

And Capote's "My Side of the Matter":

> I know what is being said about me and you can take my side or theirs, that's your own business. It's my word against Eunice's and Olivia-Ann's, and it should be plain enough to anyone with two good eyes which one of us has their wits about them. I just want the citizens of the U.S.A. to know the facts, that's all.

Truman Capote knew—with the insightfulness of the writer who wishes not to be one sometimes and can step aside and see what his or her function as a writer means to others—that photographs were more immediate and vital than words and would eventually be more attractive to the general reading audience. And as a fashionable person, he saw attractiveness as the barometer of morality. (Recall his on-the-air feud with Jacqueline Susann, author of *Valley of the Dolls.* Capote described her appearance as not unlike that of "a truck driver in drag," a curious statement, layered like an onion. The truck driver as sometime homosexual erotic artifact; drag as part of the [then] homosexual code or underground; a truck driver in drag being, perhaps, of interest to Truman Capote only as an image of humor. With this comment he was spitting in the face of America for its acceptance of what he could not see as a "real" woman—someone successful as an author—and its rejection of the "real" one—himself. His joke empowered him, made him greater than the woman America seemed to prefer, Jacqueline Susann.)

Truman Capote's travel book, *Local Color* (1949), with accompanying photographic essays by Karl Bissinger, Cecil Beaton, and so on, was an attempt to conjoin his writing with the photographic demands of publicity. "My prettiest book, inside and out," he wrote to John Malcolm Brinnin.

Before 1947, illustrations in the form of watercolors by Eugene Berman, Christian Berard, and the like were used, mostly, to represent authors. Truman Capote single-handedly created a new interpretation of photography for his audience. Thereafter, photographs—of the bodies that created the words—were used to sell words.

Eudora Welty, who, in the '30s and '40s, took photographs for the WPA project, also photographed Katherine Anne Porter (on whom Capote modeled Alice Lee Langman in *Answered Prayers*). The difference between the photographs of Katherine Anne Porter and Capote's authoress photograph is this: Porter is beautiful and therefore a *removed* object; Capote is sexual and simply embodies the subtext of his first book. *Other Voices, Other Rooms* is an idea about femininity made palpable by Capote's shallow interpretation.

Only one woman author—not as famous as Capote—equaled the power of his 1947 photograph: Jane Bowles in Karl Bissinger's portrait, taken in 1946 to accompany a story of hers that appeared in *Harper's Bazaar*. Bowles's photograph *is* a reinterpretation of what Capote projected in 1947. It illustrates the idea that femininity, as an idea, does fuck you up.

Jane Bowles, "that genius imp, that laughing, hilarious, tortured elf," was one woman author—a Jew, a lesbian, not a maiden aunt—from whom Capote tried to steal but could not. He attempted to retranslate her aesthetic—language and speech as unrepresentative of a woman's internal life, humor as the best way to represent the garishness of internal life in general—in his script for John Huston's film *Beat the Devil*. In it, Jennifer Jones plays Bowles (under the name Gwendolyn) and speaks with Bowles's syntax. "Isn't that what we're most interested in: sin?" she inquires, just as Bowles had written to a friend, "There's nothing original about me but a little original sin."

Gwendolyn's loopy rationale ("I told him that I was in love with you when I thought you were dead. . . . It made you seem less dead") is also reminiscent of Bowles's fiction; Christina Goering in *Two Serious Ladies*, for example: "'Oh, I can't tell you, my dear, how sorry I am,' said Miss Goering, taking both his hands in hers and pressing them to her lips. . . . 'I can't tell you how these gloves remind me of my childhood,' Miss Goering continued."

Jane Bowles wrote of Capote in a letter to her husband Paul: "Alice T[oklas] was delighted that you didn't really care for him very much. . . . She doesn't seem to worry in the least, however, about my liking him. So I'm insulted . . . again." Bowles did not consider Capote a woman. Her interest in the female body specifically precluded her complicity in Capote's self-delusion. Her very noncomplicity may explain why one of the few truly laudatory pieces Capote ever wrote about a woman was his introduction to her *Collected Work*, completed in 1966, shortly after the publication of *In Cold Blood* and Capote's reversion to manhood: "Mrs. Bowles, by virtue of her talent and the strange visions it enclose[s], and

Katherine Ann Porter; photograph by Eudora Welty.

Jane Bowles

because of her personality's startling blend of playful-puppy candor and feline sophistication, [is] an imposing, stage-front presence."

Realizing the authenticity behind Jane Bowles's "feline sophistication" was the end, too, of Capote's career as a woman author. There was no way *into* that sophistication without being literally exposed to women. Jane Bowles's physical proximity to women was not something Capote could experience. And his anger, fear, and resentment of this fact led to the self-caricature he projected in the film *Murder by Death*, and his unforgiving descriptions of any man he did not consider one—like Rusty Trawler, the millionaire, in *Breakfast at Tiffany's*, who was also a portrait of the physically confused woman Truman Capote eventually became:

[Rusty] was a middle-aged child that had never shed its baby fat, though some gifted tailor had almost succeeded in camouflaging his plump and spankable bottom. There wasn't a suspicion of bone in his body; his face, a zero filled in with pretty miniature features, had an unused, a virginal quality: it was as if he'd been born, then expanded, his skin remaining unlined as a blown-up balloon, and his mouth, though ready for squalls and tantrums, a spoiled sweet puckering.

The above description presaged the familiar television image of Truman Capote in later years: a series of circles to be filled in by the imagination. Although his distinct, inimitable voice interfered with this imaginative process, Capote, like Rusty Trawler, could not, eventually, commit to what he had become. As Holly Golightly said, "Can't you see it's just that Rusty feels safer in diapers than he would in a skirt? . . . He tried to stab me with a butter knife because I told him to grow up and face the issue, settle down and play house with a nice fatherly truck driver," a statement that recalls Jacqueline Susann, the truck driver with whom Truman Capote could not play at all.

Writing of a woman (Jane Bowles) without malice, Truman Capote saw himself, in comparison, as a man: the author of a book (*In Cold Blood*) about vanity turned to pain and grief and the taking of life, life lived as a man. *In Cold Blood* is, above all, Truman Capote's expression of his sadness at being a man, at the juncture writing creates between the self we see and the self we cannot know, that neither words nor photographs can ever accurately record. *In Cold Blood* is a book replete with this image question. Perry Smith is consumed by the idea of his face's meaning, construction, and story; it is like language to him and to Capote. *In Cold Blood* is an examination of the way in which the traditional values associated with women—concern with appearance as it tells a story to the world—are adopted "naturally" by a man:

Time rarely weighed upon [Perry] for he had many ways of passing it—among them, mirror-gazing. [. . .] his own face enthralled him. Each angle of it induced a different impression. It was a changeling's face, and mirror-guided experiments had taught him how to ring the changes, how to look ominous, now impish, now soulful; a tilt of the head, a twist of the lips, and the corrupt gypsy became the gentle romantic.

In 1948, Capote went to Paris. "My book's succès fou there," he told John Malcolm Brinnin. "Why shouldn't *I* be?" In 1949, he also went to North Africa, where he became reacquainted with "that modern legend" Jane Bowles. A photograph was taken of them somewhere in Tangier. Capote is heavier than he was in 1947. Bowles is already whatever she meant to be. She is directing her smile, her complete attention, which she equated with affection, toward Capote, who seems to be considering whether or not to accept this attention. In that moment, which appears to be a long one, Truman Capote began making his long move away from women, becoming closer still.

Untitled

To know the fullness of
the weight of time,

                    hugely
dispersed   & gathered simultaneously,

           enormous
as the sun's gold (we had forgotten)
on this winter evening —

                       the size, the color
of that gathering hung on
the very edge of our horizon, touching it
barely,   deep, deep gold,

                           the cloud-streaks
gray, blue-green, mauve darkening,
spread into distance either side of it,
stretched away but clinging
back for warmth, moving reluctantly
away.   We had forgotten it:
the brightness, roundness of it,   there to
light us, there to heat the world, to be also
magnificent,   a god,   a wonder,
the heart-core of us, turned now
toward us,

           untouchable —
the huge shout tempered for
our hearing,   gigantic
in offering,

             so none of our words can

reach to it.
          We are shadows
beneath it,   move numbly backward
& forward, with barely a direction, under the weight of
that fullness,   dazed, uncertain
how to follow,
          wishing
to come closer,   pressed by the fullness of time,
            less than
the earth that stirs, stirs with it,
the earth that rustles.

The
End

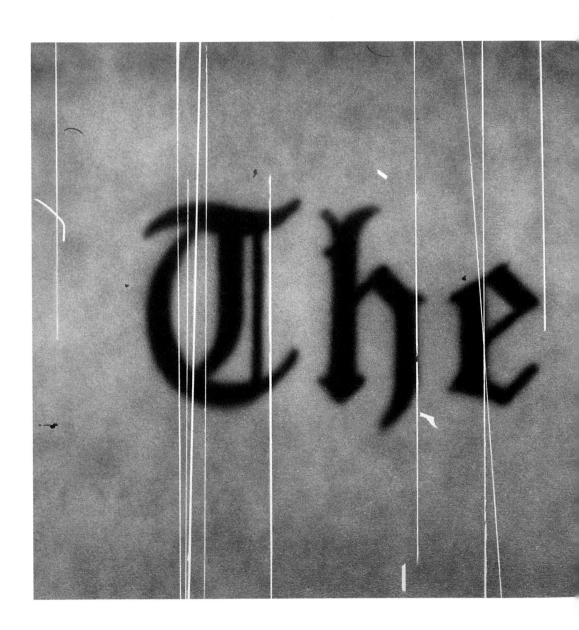

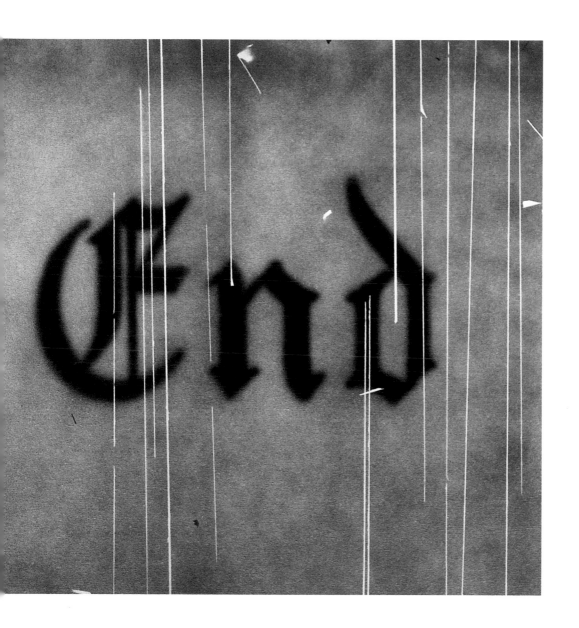

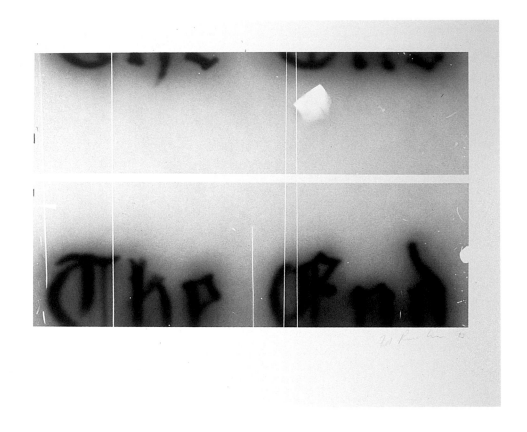

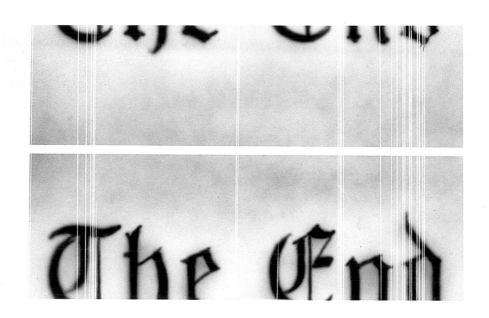

The End

Once, many years ago, American Pop culture created a space—on the screen, on the road, in your dreams—where you could slough off the encumbrances of place and time, the baggage of identity, and . . . be free. Pop Art, thirty years ago, tried to merge high and low in a similarly beautifully accessible poem of absolute freedom. The darkness was always there—the film noir alleyway leading to The Factory as was the High Art resistance, but the light of general prosperity buoyed hope and kept the darkness where it belonged, at the margins, *In Cold Blood*, on Richard Speck's arm, on Charlie Manson's forehead.

Fast forward to 1994: boy, is that dream over! Tabloidism—the obsession with turning over every rock, ferreting out every snake, and exonerating every snake as a holy victim—has poisoned the American Pop dream. Margin has become mainstream: darkness itself is in the spotlight.

Edward Ruscha, having learned from Las Vegas how to turn the dream of Pop to a logo on the horizon, or to a word to contain the energy of the moment, having also found the *informe* in information and the la-la in L.A., has always known something of the onset of darkness. At the end of the Pop era (and of the century), Ruscha's art, and particularly *The End*—well, I wouldn't be an art critic if I didn't say it—plays an endgame for Pop. And cliché aside, Ruscha's art projects the remains of the day in a format that is in tune to the flow of meaning at the end of things.

The End raises to the level of art a type of lettering that was auxiliary to an art form (film) whose use-value was so exploited during its market lifetime that it can only now, in its afterlife, migrate to other fields of meaning and become true art. The letters—taken from the final credits of an old movie—suggest the kind of entropy that leads "late" art to dwell on the end of the art form (the same entropy that made the Beatles, for example, put out their best songs ["Hey Jude, na, na, na, na"] after they were technically over). The art from which this title comes is itself too much to take, too corny, too full of memory, too embarrassing, too painful. Better to avoid the trauma of memory by fetishizing its marginal elements.

Ruscha's letterings in *The End* revel in the minute pleasures of the "redressed imagination," which does the long-term dreamwork of culture by squeezing meaning out of intractable kitsch material that the passage of time has impacted in remakes and reruns. His letterings shine with a dull bad-print, old-movie glow, like light from the dead star called Hollywood Babylon. Rewatching this movie now, the mind weaves a desire path of meaning over the fissures and faults, the dated aspects and technical glitches. The redressed imagination says, You don't need high art: better to be a couch potato and eke a comforting meaning, in digestible doses, out of a very slowly eroding (or, if it becomes a classic, hardening) husk of market reification.

Ruscha's *The End* exists at the end of such a movie cycle, where nuance meets its vanishing point and turns back. He dwells on imperfections as though they create new meaning. As though they will finally help us get over it or get on with it. The glitches play highly abstracted games of titillation, itching the self-consciousness that afflicts all late art with hints of other options, of roads not taken, of lives to be lived, still. In this, the device compares to the movie gambit of showing action occurring within a movie theater (in *Saboteur* or *Manhattan Murder Mystery*), or in the projection booth (*The Blob*, original and remake, or *Desperately Seeking Susan*). Ruscha's titled titles exist at the same crisis point as these scenes where a hole is punched through the screen or the film burned: they attempt to steady the rickety-ness that comes from a self-conscious art form by absorbing it in a violent interruption. Ruscha has always probed the gaps in culture, in communication, in the world, in the space between you and me. With *The End* he seems to have reached a point of redress where the gaps pile up and break, knocking the message off kilter. Most fateful of all, then, I can't help but see these works as signs at the end of a dream, a culture. Ruscha alone of the artists who were there at the beginning of the Big Pop seems interested in witnessing the pop of the Pop at the end of the era.

—Robert Mahoney

Tuesday Evening

She plundered the fun in his hair.
The others were let go.
There was a wet star on the stair.
Outside it had decided to snow.

Not everyone gets off at this stop
the turtlelike conductor said.
If you'd like to hear those beans hop
it could be arranged in your head.

Now from every side, cheerleaders
and their disc-eyed boyfriends come.
The latter put up bird feeders.
Birds alight on them and are dumb

with anticipation of the meal.
The punishment is not due
in our time said the wise old eel.
Its overture is still distant in the blue

sign of the ruined factory. You'll know
when it starts up. Darn! That's what I thought
it would be, I said. Isn't there a hoe
somewhere to root these weeds out?

Or a chair on a blanket
of a manor house in time
and shouldn't we somehow thank it
for the perfection of the climb?

Straight over roads, in culottes
the marching women go. Why besmirch
that casket, choose fleshpots
over a stand of young birch?

The veranda failed to make an impression,
ditto the lavaliere.
Potted ferns have become my obsession,
waltzing under the chandelier.

No one weeps to me anymore.
Then up and spake greengrocer Fred:
"Time and love are a whore
and after the news there is bed

to take to. Don't you agree?
It's lonely to believe, but it's half
the fun. Here, take a pee
on me, but over there by that calf."

The things we thought of naming
are crystals now. You can see from the porte cochere
now a small business flaming,
now the besotted rind of some pear.

It all seems ages ago—that time
of not being able to choose
or think of a rhyme
for "so many books to peruse

until the body is done." A chicken
might pass by and never notice
us standing pale as a mannequin,
clutching a fistful of myosotis

as though this would matter some day to some lover
when the time was ripe and our mooring
had been sliced. Then it would be time to rediscover
a plashing that would seem more alluring

for being ancient. You see, the past
never happened. Nothing can survive long in its heady
embrace. Our memories are a simulcast
of lost conventions, already

drowning in their sleep. In some such
wise we outgrew ourselves, lianas
over lichen. Forasmuch
as sweetness comes to the nicotianas

only at evening, your arrangement is overbred,
threadbare. You may want to think about this
a little. Down in their pavilion, whose overfed
airs waft lightly, naughtily, Dad and Sis

are waving, calling your name, over
and over again. But it's like a wall of veil
tipped in. We can dance only alone. Rover
senses an advantage—it's the Airedale

from the next block again. To keep even the peace
sounds extraneous, now. How many senses
do we need? Our motives predecease
our cashing them in. Fences

will be happy to relieve you of that icon
for a small consideration. And you,
what about you? Slowly unraveling, the chaconne
sizes us up: right pew,

wrong church. O if ever the devil
comes to claim his due, let it be after
the touching ceremony, yet before the revel
becomes frenzied, and ambitions turn to laughter.

Resist, friends, that last day's dying.
The melodious mode obtains. Always
remember that. At trying
moments, practice the art of paraphrase.

Just because someone hands you something of value
don't imagine you're in it for the money.
You can always tell a gal-pal you
prefer the snakeroot's scented hegemony.

Or go for a walk. It counts too.
In my charming madness I dress plainer
than when they used to mispronounce you,
but what's correct streetwear in N'Djamena

clashes in the old upstate classroom.
Come, we're weak enough to share a posset,
divide with the boys another hecatomb.
All other rodomontades are strictly bullshit.

Such are the passwords that tired Aeneas
wept for outside the potting shed,
when, face pressed to the pane, he sought Linnaeus'
sage advice. And the farm turned over a new leaf instead.

We can't resist; we're all thumbs, it seems,
when it comes to grasping mantras.
The oxen are waiting for us downstream; academe's
no place for botanizing, and the tantra's

closed to us. Song and voice, piano and flowers,
abduct us to their plateau.
Look—becalmed, a horse devours
crocuses in the ruts by an old chateau.

If this is about being regal, it must be Japan
has assented. Let's take the vaporetto
to where it goes. A sea cucumber of marzipan
promises decorum. The boatman quaffs Amaretto.

Well, and this is the way I've always done it. A fricative
voice from the valley wants to think so. Those jars of ointment
are still untouched. Were patients always so uncommunicative?
Even Jeremy? He's late for his appointment,

and I must go down an inclined plane
to the city's anthill, with only dissolved rage
for company. And should some perdurable chatelaine
push the envelope, must we summon the archimage

to bandage the hurt? Only a little moisture
remains at the tip of the tongue, a pro forma
signal of engagement. Before the great rupture,
still a duo, we sang the "Casta Diva" from *Norma*

on Sunday morning. Now all's retrograde;
the new openness cloys. Pencils are to sharpen,
yet I keep mine dull. My cockade
is tarnished, my dress puny, my shoes of cordovan

behind the bed. Sometimes I like to ride in a carriage,
over dales and downs. My fiancée is a lacrosse player.
When the moon is full one's in the mood for marriage,
amiable for awhile. But the village soothsayer

warned us against it, of dreary days to come
unless we interacted on a vast scale. And who can predict
furtive new developments? Because we'd swum
the Hellespont long ago, in our youth, we assumed the verdict

would be sealed by now. And you know, only anonymous
lovers seem to make it to the altar. The rest are branded
with a time and place, and rarely know each other. The eponymous
host of the Bridge and Barrel, a moralist, was openhanded,

yet nothing could bar the tear from one blue eye. He'd chattered
vainly till now. So I assumed the aggressor's fate.
Behind the door crockery clattered
mysteriously, the beadle was stunned, the boilerplate

contract wilted in the intense heat
of the deluged afternoon. Even when the tumbrel
arrived, it seemed it would have to wait
for the century to catch up. Meanwhile, in the adumbral

hall not a whistle could be heard, no screams, no catcalls,
unless you counted the willows' sobbing.
Evening came on boisterous. Pirouettes and pratfalls
were executed before an admiring crowd. Demons were hobnobbing

with whatever entered on skis. To have proffered
only this was sublimely sufficient. But what of cattails
loosing seeds on the air like milkweed? A scoffer'd
not turn away, just this once, for what prevails

is most certainly what will be current
years from now: celadon pods with opal juices
oozing from them. Fruits of the sand, blackcurrant
and bayberry, and a crowd of mild smiles, a burnoose's

wandering cord. When needed to combat flatulence,
the correct pills turn up in pairs. I mistook embroidery
in the stair carpet for something else, the doll's petulance
for a sign from the heavens. The whole dang menagerie

is after me now; I have strength for but one curtain call,
and that a swift one. But will the critics
recite my reasons? Luckily a landfall
materialized in the nick of time. Luckily my desire wasn't great. Politics

overwhelms us all. In seasons of strife we compose palinodes
against the breakers, retracting what was lithe
in our believing. By evening, its heresy implodes
under an August moon; repercussions writhe

in a context of mangroves. Perfervid scroungers
invade the Catalog Fulfillment Center, diverting the sick energy
in our wake into easeful light, and day. A few loungers
on the mezzanine are puzzled, but most are not. The ambient lethargy

incises its monogram on the walls of bathhouses, in wooden
tunnels: to wit, man plays a role in his conspiracy,
ergo, he cannot be a victim. After a sudden
denouement, the climate again turns bland; its apostasy

was too minute to register on God's barometer.
Only an occasional letter to the *Times*
hinted that a change might have occurred.
Otherwise it was *beau fixe* on the speedometer

as it raced toward clayey lands with windmills
and similar giddy appurtenances. From far,
from night and morning, innovations arrive in schools, whippoorwills
are calling. The Circolo Italiano welcomes new adherents, a streetcar

bearing members of the Supreme Court floats in the sky like a zeppelin.
It was all over in a trance. Now it's the fiction
weighs us down, like an iron corset. Adrenaline
is channeled into new, virtuoso ways, wherein constriction

is viewed as normal, soothing as an antimacassar.
Better to live in a fictive aura, I say, than putter
in one's garden forever, praying to NASA
at dusk, as in Millet's *Angelus,* closing a shutter

on substantive dreaming. That, after all, is where we're
at. It is time for the rebuilding of melody
on a grand scale. Reread Shakespeare; a fakir here
and there won't sabotage the kernel of parody

baked into the airiest ontological *mille-feuilles,* nor change that gold
back into straw. The medicine men knew what they were doing when
they lanced boils with direct imaging. Charm gained a foothold,
then exploded into bronze deities. No matter, the regimen

practiced by the ancients, i.e., inhaling
dust and air near a body of water, is still around to restore
lost fossils of wit to their living, vibrant selves, unveiling
a menu both familiar and alluring. Before

quitting this backdrop of a Renaissance piazza, open
your body and mind to all comers. They are both factory and garden
to the happy few, thunderstorms to some, a dull weapon
though fierce, to others. And as attitudes harden,

the lost light stares as a man in pyjamas
crosses the ravaged street. All this decision-making entails
sophomoric stunts and impatience. From the Bahamas
to Torquay stretches the dim pilgrimage. Cocktails

infiltrate it, but the man knows he must go
just so far and stop, that his beloved will have forgotten
him by then. He must choose the stars or the snow,
a naked stick figure. All the rotten

things that can befall a man with a comb and toothbrush
already happened to him, leagues ago. And there is no ending
it. Yet the past is profitless slush,
same as the present. Tomorrow is on hold, pending,

and great lizards infiltrate the Dalmatian-spotted
sky. Was it for this you gave yourself up
to some cause or other, that has now trickled away, dotted
with colored pom-poms? Only a final hiccup

sits on the step, awaiting orders. You were wrong about language,
see. Its arrows are raining down like ejected porcupine
quills. An archer (Robin Hood, for instance) could gauge
the correct distance between identical hummocks. Which is fine

with me, except I don't think anybody's going to notice
the directive that brought you here. Best to marshal the
secondary promptings and forget the awful journey before rigor mortis
sets in. You mean it hasn't? Right. Then I'm still in the Marshalsea,

my dependency shall never cease! And there's a kind of happiness,
though a bitter one, in that. I'm going to cash in my chips
and quit while I'm winning. The loveliness
of statues of statesmen survives, a barcarolle drips

from their sagging jaws, graphic as springtime.
In twos and threes, peasants
vanish behind yon ridge. The celestial pantomime
engulfs them slowly. The pheasants

of our kingdom aren't as plump as yours. No matter.
I'll wager a microclimate's responsible. And did your sister
ever loan you those three bucks? No, the regatta
closed down while we were still ogling its pinnaces, and a twister

slashed through at that precise moment, there was nowhere
to hide, in the confusion we got separated.
Now I must arise and go where
the flying fishes play, and poppies perplex the cultivated

plain. Go ahead, I'll keep an eye on things, you can breathe
easy. It's what I had in mind: a sail printed all over
with musical staves. I would unsheathe
love's whippet and embrace us all, even if Rover

never growled again. "Springs, when they happen, happen elsewhere.
A certain sexiness . . . ," ventured the prince. But where, oh where, is the nectar
that makes babes of us? Our printout's in disrepair,
the parterres are fading, and the projector

is spinning out of control. Half a hundred youths
could sustain us, swimming in the moat
with reeds to breathe through. The vacant booths
by the front gate are cheerless indeed. A stoat

swept by me on the waters, halfway to refurbished oblivion,
but my antennae suggest nothing apposite
to formalize his trajectory. A safe-conduct from the Bolivian
chargé d'affaires flutters in the breeze of my room. In the windows opposite

a massacre is reflected. Is it meant as a codicil,
or mere free-form tangling? Anyway, night is serendipitous
again; swallows clutter my windowsill,
and bats are executing stately arabesques. A precipitous

slide into belief must have occurred recently, but left no earnest
of its passing. A videotape of sports bloopers
keeps unreeling, determined to rescue its syllabus from the furnace
of eternity; airheads are treated roughly. One of those Victorian peasoupers

is equalizing everything, titmouse and pterodactyl
alike. When it will be the fashion again we'll have trochees
galore. Even the bellicose double dactyl
will flourish for a time, in Okefenokees

of subjectivity. Lakes will overflow, bargain
counters shrivel to nothing, the Great Bear look away, brittle
talismans explode at dormer windows. The degradation Ruskin
warned against is back, a heap of frozen spittle.

We see one thing next to another. In time they get superimposed,
and then who looks silly? Not us, as you might think, but the curve
we are plotted on, head to head, a parabola in the throes
of vomiting its formula, piqued by the sullen verve

of day, while night is siphoned off again. And as wolverines
prefer Michigan, so this civil branch of holly is nailed to your door, lest you
fear my coming, or any uncourteous declaiming, or submarines
in the bay that spreads before us, or any gumshoe.

We'll party when the millennium gets closer. Meanwhile
I wanted to mention your feet. A dowser
could locate your contentedness zone. But where have you been while
folkdancing broke out, and colorful piñatas, waking Bowser

in his kennel, rendering the last victuals
in the larder unappetizing? Yet those feet shall impose the glory
of my slogans on the unsuspecting world that belittles
them now, but shall whistle them *con amore*

anon. That doesn't mean "peace at any price,"
but a shaking-down of old, purblind principles
that were always getting in the way. Self-sacrifice
will be on the agenda, a lowering of expectations, a ban on municipal

iron fences and picnics. Man must return to his earth,
experience its seasons, frosts, its labyrinthine
processes, the spectacle of continual rebirth
in one's own time. Only then will the sunshine

each weekday bears in its quiver expand till the vernal
equinox rounds it off, then subtracts a little more each day,
though always leaving a little, even in hyperboreal climes where eternal
ice floes fringe the latitudes. On a beautiful day in May

you might forget this, but there it is, always creeping up on you.
Permit me then for the umpteenth time to reiterate
that basking in the sun like an otter or curlew
isn't the whole story. Tomorrow may obliterate

your projects and belongings, casting a shadow longer than the equator
into your private sector, to wit, your plan to take a hovercraft
across the lagoon and have lunch there, leaving the waiter
a handsome tip. For though your garrison be fully staffed,

the near future, like an overcrowded howdah,
trumpets its imminent arrival, opens the floodgate
of a thousand teeming minor ills, spoiling the chowder
and marching society's annual gymkhana, letting in smog to asphyxiate

palms and eucalyptuses. One paddles in the backwash of the present,
laughing at its doodles, unpinning its robes,
smoothing its ribbons, and lo and behold an unpleasant
emu is blocking the path; its one good eye probes

your premises and tacit understandings, and the outing
is postponed till another day. Or you could be reclining
on a rock like Fra Diavolo and have it sneak up on you, spouting
praise for the way the city looks after a shower, divining

its outer shallows from the number of storm windows
taken down and stashed away, for it has the shape of a sonata—
bent, unyielding. And, once it's laid out in windrows,
open to the difficult past, that of a fish on a platter.

Expect no malice from it and freshets
will foam, gathering strength as they leapfrog the mountain.
But a quieter realism plumbs the essence of ponds, while nitwits
worship the machine-tooled elegies of the fountain,

that wets its basin and the nearby grass. In a moment the dustmen
will be here, and in the time remaining it behooves
me to insist again on the lust men
invent, then cherish. But since my mistress disapproves,

I'll toe the line. And should you ask me why, sir,
I'll say it's because one's sex drives are like compulsive handwashing:
better early on in life than late. Yet I'm still spry, sir,
though perhaps no longer as dashing

as in times gone by, and can wolf down the elemental conundrum
in one gulp—its "How different one feels after doing something:
calm, and in a calm way almost tragic; in any case far from the unwholesome
figure we cut in the reveries of others, a rum thing

not fit to be seen in public with." Yet it is this ominous Bedouin
whose contours blur when someone glimpses
us, and is what we are remembered as, for no one can see our genuine
side falling to pieces all down our declamatory gestures. They treat pimps as

equals, ignoring all shortcomings save ours. And of course, no commerce
is possible between these two noncommunicating vessels of our being. As
    urushiol
is to poison ivy, so is our own positive self-image the obverse
of all that will ever be said and thought about us, the vitriol

we gargle with in the morning, just as others do. This impasse
does, however, have an escape clause written into it: planned
enhancements, they call it. So that if one *is* knocked flat on his ass
by vile opprobrium, he need only consult his pocket mirror: the sand

will seem to flow upwards through the hourglass; one is pickled
in one's own humors, yet the dismantled ideal
rescued from youth is still pulsing, viable, having trickled
from the retort of self-consciousness into the frosted vial

of everyone's singular consciousness noting it's the same
as all the others, with one vital difference: it belongs to no one.
Thus a few may climb several steps above the crowd, achieve fame
and personal fulfillment in a flaring instant, sing songs to one

more beloved than the rest, yet still cherish the charm and quirkiness
that entangle all individuals in the racemes
of an ever-expanding Sargasso Sea whose murkiness
comes at last to seem exemplary. Thus, between two extremes

hidden in blue distance, the dimensionless
regions of the self do have their day. We like this, that,
and the other; have our doubts about certain things; enjoy pretension less
than we did when we were young; are not above throwing out a caveat

or two; and in a word are comfortable in the saddle
reality offers to each of her children, simultaneously
convincing each of us we're superior, that no one else could straddle
her mount as elegantly as we. And when, all extraneously,

the truth erupts, and we find we are but one of an army of supernumeraries
raising spears to salute the final duet
between our ego and the endlessly branching itineraries
of our *semblables,* a robed celebrant is already raising the cruet

of salve to anoint the whole syndrome. And it's their proper
perspective that finally gets clamped onto things and us, including
our attitudes, hopes, half-baked ambitions, psychoses: everything an
	eavesdropper
already knows about us, along with the clothes we wear and the brooding

interiors we inhabit. It's getting late; the pageant
oozes forward, act four is yet to come, and so is dusk.
Still, ripeness must soon be intuited; a sealant
freeze the tragic act under construction. Let's husk

the ear of its plenitude, forget additional worries,
let Mom and apple pie go down the tubes, if indeed
that's their resolve. For, satisfying as it is to fling a pot, once the slurry's
reached the proper consistency, better still is it to join the stampede

away from it once it's finished. Which, as of now,
it is. Wait a minute! You told us eternal flux
was the ordering principle here, and in the next breath you disavow
open-endedness. What kind of clucks

do you take us for, anyway? Everyone knows that once something's finished,
decay sets in. But we were going to outwit all that. So
where's your panacea now? The snake oil? Smoke and mirrors? Diminished
expectations can never supplant the still-moist, half-hesitant tableau

we thought to be included in, and to pursue
our private interests and destinies in, till doomsday. Well, I
never said my system was foolproof. You did too! I did not. Did too!
Did not. Did too. Did not. Did too. Hell, I

only said let's wait a while and see what happens, maybe
something will, and if it doesn't, well, our personal
investment in the thing hasn't been that enormous, you crybaby;
we can still emerge unscathed. These are exceptional

times, after all. And all along I thought I was pointed
in the right direction, that if I just kept my seat
I'd get to a destination. I knew the instructions were disjointed,
garbled, but imagined we'd eventually make up the lost time. Yet one deadbeat

can pollute a whole universe. The sensuous green mounds
I'd been anticipating are nowhere to be seen. Instead, a dull
urban waste reveals itself, vistas of broken masonry, out of bounds
to the ordinary time-traveler. How, then, did he lull

us, me and the others, into signing on for the trip?
By exposing himself, and pretending
not to see. Solar wind sandpapers the airstrip,
while only a few hundred yards away, bending

hostesses coddle stranded voyagers with canapés
and rum punch. To have had this in the early stage,
not the earliest, but the one right after the days
began to shorten imperceptibly! And one's rage

was a good thing, good for oneself and even
for others, at that critical juncture. Dryness
of the mouth was seldom a problem. Winking asides would leaven
the dullest textbook. Your highness

knows all this, yet if she will but indulge
my wobbling fancies a bit longer, I'll . . . Where was I? Oh, and then
a great hurricane came, and took away the leaves. The bulge
in the calceolaria bush was gone. By all the gods, when

next I saw him, he was gay, gay as any jackanapes. Is
this really what you had in mind, I asked.
But he merely smiled and replied, "None of your biz,"
and walked out onto the little peninsula and basked

as though he meant it. And in a funny kind of way, the nifty
feeling of those years has returned. I can't explain it,
but perhaps it means that once you're over fifty
you're rid of a lot of decibels. You've got a tiger; so unchain it

and then see what explanations they give. Walk through
your foot to the place behind it, the air
will frizz your whiskers. You're still young enough to talk through
the night, among friends, the way you used to do somewhere.

An alphabet is forming words. We who watch them
never imagine pronouncing them, and another opportunity
is missed. You must be awake to snatch them—
them, and the scent they give off with impunity.

We all tagged along, and in the end there was nothing
to see—nothing and a lot. A lot in terms of contour, texture,
world. That sort of thing. The real fun and its clothing.
You can forget that. Next, you're

planning a brief trip. Perhaps a visit to Paul Bunyan
and Babe, the blue ox. There's time now. Piranhas
dream, at peace with themselves and with the floating world. A grunion
slips nervously past. The heat, the stillness are oppressive. Iguanas . . .

Uncle Ed

Well, it looks like the plumbing in the house is shot entirely to hell. The toilet won't flush and foul matter backs up into the bathtub. The plumber finally came and had a look at it. Now he's prowling around out in the mulberry grove over the cesspool. I don't know what he expects to find there. I let him take his own good time. Besides, there's no way to hurry him. His manner is to sit and smoke, with no regard for the glue and grease he carries about on his person. He has brown teeth. His face is grizzled. In his speech the topics of sewage and fishing prevail. It was from him I learned the two primary rules of plumbing: shit won't run uphill, and Saturday night is payday.

While he fiddled with the toilet tank he spoke to me in parables about his two jobs of the day before. He was called to a factory to clear the clogged toilets. The factory employs only women, to sew women's underclothes. "These ladies," he says, "sit on their butts all day. They don't do anything to keep their bowels moving. Turds as long as your arm." He illustrated with his own brawny forearm. "It stifles the flow," he said. "Then they called me to the school. The toilets in the home economics room were plugged up. Those girls eat candy and cookies all day. You can't imagine the turds that come out of those little girls. It's a wonder it doesn't ruin their health, give them piles, mess up their assholes. I had to go outside and take up the tile covering the sewer line. The principal came along and got hysterical when he saw a bloody napkin float by. He called the superintendent over. They both got a big kick out of it. These young girls are ashamed to show they're bleeding, so they throw the napkins in the commode instead of the trashcan."

There was a long pause in which the only sound was the rustle of paper as he rolled a cigarette. He spoke as he lit up. "Mabry died last week you know. It was in the paper." I said I didn't know. He went on. "His wife took sick with lung disease. She was doing poorly at home so they put her in a sanatorium. Mabry took it hard. Drew his money out of the bank, went on a spree for three weeks, then died in his room surrounded by fifty empty whiskey bottles." "Like his pa," I said. "Yeah, Ed had the weakness too," he said. "That's not the half of it," I said. There was another long pause. The plumber wasn't saying anything, he just sat there looking at me. He was waiting for me to start in. So I started in.

Uncle Ed was a poor shot. But that didn't stop him from hunting in the swamp with the rest of us for deer, coon, and the rare panther or bobcat. Camp was the only place he could drink in peace. Aunt Clara was a teetotaler and gave him ten kinds of hell if she caught him boozing. Camp was where he did his heavy drinking. I took a slug now and then to get the smell on my breath and act the fool, but Uncle Ed drank in earnest. During the day he was never far from a jug, and at night when he thought everyone was asleep he took drinks on the sly, getting more than his due. Tom caught him at it three nights running, but didn't say anything.

The last day out was hard on Uncle Ed. His thirst gained in desperation as the supply dwindled. Needing a deer to justify spending all that time away from home doing nothing but drinking and hunting, the rest of us fanned out to look for game. Uncle Ed volunteered to stay behind to scour the pots. That's what he said, but really he just wanted to stay close to the last remaining jug. Late in the day we came back empty-handed to find him in high spirits, bragging in his rambling alcoholic fashion about a rendezvous he may or may not have had with Mary Barnes sometime in the past twenty years. He hadn't done a thing about washing the dishes, which still lay filthy in a tub of greasy water.

The whiskey was barely holding out, but we all managed to get drunk before bedding down. When Uncle Ed staggered out of the tent for a piss, Tom replaced the whiskey jug with a jug of coal oil, hiding the booze under his gear. Half an hour later we all watched as Uncle Ed slipped from his pallet in the dark and made his way on all fours toward the jug. He pulled the cork and turned it up. An eternity of perhaps two seconds passed before he spewed and began to choke, horrible noises issuing from his throat. He stumbled outside and stuck his head full down into the tub of filthy dishwater, taking deep draughts. We had some fun out of him. He sulled up and wouldn't talk to us.

He was still sulling the next morning when we broke camp. We were almost out of the swamp on the edge of town when a deer ran right at us. Uncle Ed took his usual shaky shot and missed, but Tom brought it down with a gut shot. We looked it over. The deer was slashed and bleeding on its flanks and neck. We figured it for a scrape with a bobcat. Our bunch rode jubilantly into town with our prize, right into a large crowd in front of the bank. They went wild when they saw the gashes in the deer's hide. It was identified as the deer that moments before had jumped through the bank's plate-glass window. Apparently lost and confused in the street, the bewildered animal had tried to escape into the trees reflected in the glass. It burst through into the midst of tellers and depositors and sent them fleeing in one body out the front door. Splashing blood from its wounds, the deer had then broken through the door to the president's office, where it overturned chairs and scattered the morning mail. After a quarter minute of destruction, the president managed to shout the deer out the open alley door and from there it made its escape into the swamp, where we stumbled on it.

The deer had been preceded out the alley door by Aunt Clara. She was Uncle Ed's second wife. His first wife, Flora, had borne him two children and then fell into a decline that culminated in her interment. On her deathbed she made her younger sister Clara promise to marry Uncle Ed and raise the children. Clara did it. She married Uncle Ed, raised the children, and with these actions considered herself to have fulfilled her obligation to her dead sister. As far as any other marital duties went, she displayed little interest in Uncle Ed. In fact, his mere presence was enough to put her into a state of sensory stupefaction. On the other hand, certain men of the town knew her to be a high-spirited and abundantly willing woman. And indeed it was while in the company of the bank president and while enjoying his usurious embraces that the two had been surprised in a state of undress by the panicked deer. As the deer stormed around the office Aunt Clara flew out the back door, pausing in the alley to gather, lace, and button her displaced garments. Inside, the president could only shout at the deer and not run after it, being incommoded by having his pants down around his ankles. This happy circumstance perhaps saved his life as it restrained his natural courage and kept him from toppling flush into the deer's furious path. Aunt Clara escaped in the opposite direction from the deer, which was followed at a distance by armed citizens who paid no attention to her rapidly receding figure behind them.

In fact, of all the multitude that witnessed the drama, it was only Uncle Ed's daughter Lena, hiding behind a tree across the alley from the bank, who saw more to the event than a desperate deer, and who saw the frantic banker and her frantic stepmother thus revealed. But the sight did not long occupy Lena's thoughts, for her purpose behind the tree was too single-minded to be diverted, even by such an otherwise signal event, for the time being at least. She was waiting for young Latham, the mechanic, to show up at his garage from his lunch hour, in order to ask him a question. To bolster his resolve in answering she carried a revolver in her handbag. A few months before, Lena had taken up the habit of dropping by the garage at the noon hour. Latham had been quick to notice her and to surmise, correctly, that she would be amenable to his advances. In short order, instead of going home to his mother's house for lunch, Latham brought it to work in a paper bag, and passed the lunch hour with Lena barricaded from prying eyes behind a wall of machinery. But after two months of these lunches Latham's enthusiasm began to wane, and he let Lena know that on some days he was obliged to go to his sick mother at noon and prepare her meal. Latham's mother's condition worsened rapidly, and Latham now had to go home every day. When Lena objected, Latham lost all patience and told her flat out not to expect to see him at the garage anymore. So this day Lena had come to await Latham's return, in order to ascertain his intentions toward her, as she believed herself several months gone with child.

Not long after Aunt Clara had disappeared down the alley, Lena was still patiently waiting behind the tree when along came the furtive figure of her brother Mabry skirting the shadows in the same direction. Mabry had spent the night with friends in a nearby town and had awakened that morning from a drunken nightmare to remember the events of the night before. Now in fear and alarm he was hurrying home to pack a bag and leave town on the afternoon train. Mabry, with a young surgeon and a farmer by the name of Gaines, had driven to the next town the previous afternoon, drinking all the way. Once arrived they continued their debauch. As night fell Gaines irritated them by trying repeatedly to get them to accompany him to the house of a woman he said he knew. Tiring of Gaines's insistence, one of the company, which had grown as the night wore on, said, "To hell with Gaines. Let's cut him." This suggestion was favorably received. Gaines, anesthetized by alcohol as thoroughly as though he had been chloroformed, was laid out on a table and the surgeon, never without his bag of instruments, cut off his balls. It was a superlative demonstration of the surgeon's art, and his care extended to properly dressing the wound before leaving Gaines to fend for himself. It was with this scene in mind that young Mabry, waking up in a strange house in a strange town, with neither Gaines nor the surgeon in evidence, fled home. Fearing recognition, he passed through the alleys. The commotion over the deer that reached him from the street only added to his apprehension, as he thought it was the tumult of a lynching party fired by the news of the outrage done to Gaines.

I fished with Gaines," the plumber said. "Hogging catfish. Gaines got down in the water and felt along the bank for a hole. When he found one he stuck his arm in. Sometimes he flushed a moccasin, sometimes an alligator snapper the size of a shoat. He lost a finger to a snapper. When he got hold of a catfish he rammed his hands into its gills and yanked it out. It cut his wrists to ribbons with the spurs on its head, thrashing from side to side like a fiend. But Gaines held on and hogged it to the shallow water where we all jumped on. We did some telephoning too. Just hook up a couple of screens to the wires of a hand-cranked generator, then drag the screens through the water and crank it up.

The fish float right to you. Big mothers too. They run sixty pounds and more." The plumber and I stared at the floor, thinking about the big fish. When it looked like he had had his say, I went on.

Uncle Ed, still sore about the coal oil and his missed shot at the deer, headed home for a drink. The carnival atmosphere of the crowd at the bank had only fanned his ill temper. Since he couldn't keep any booze in his house, he hid the stuff outside, with bottles stashed in the shrubbery, in hollow trees, and beneath the planks of the barn floor, where he also stashed the empties. His mania for burial extended to his life savings, which he had interred near a stump in the yard, not trusting banks. On winter days Uncle Ed sat in a soft chair in the front room by the window, a quilt over his legs and a pipe in his mouth, watching the spot over his money with enormous satisfaction.

Aunt Clara, in the kitchen, leaning against the back door out of breath with her head buzzing, had a great shock at the sight of Uncle Ed entering the barn. She hadn't expected him back until late in the afternoon. She ran into the bathroom and closed the door, congratulating herself as she pinned up her hair in front of the mirror on her record of successful accomplishment in her romantic intrigues. True, Uncle Ed once nearly caught her in the garden with the milkman, a sturdy lad who supplied her with milk at no charge in return for her favors, an arrangement that allowed Aunt Clara to keep for herself the money tight-fisted Uncle Ed gave her for the dairy bill. She and the young man were in the garden one night, as was their custom, and Uncle Ed was in the barn, where Aunt Clara believed him to be working at restoring the junk furniture he had filled it with. In reality he was getting drunk on moonshine in the back room, lit by a single bulb. Around that time people were going blind from drinking moonshine. Uncle Ed had the habit of closing his eyes when he drank, and the town's electrical system had this peculiarity, that at times the entire system would flicker out to blackness for a few seconds. As Uncle Ed tilted up the jug the lights went off, and when he opened his eyes there was utter darkness. Screaming "I'm going blind!" he stampeded through the barn and burst into the yard, where he discovered he could see again. At the outburst from the barn the milkman fled unseen through the hedge like a singed dog. Aunt

Clara put herself right and ran to Uncle Ed, who mumbled a story about shellac in his eyes and went to the pump to wash it out, too rattled even to wonder what Aunt Clara was doing in the garden at that time of night. Later on, when Aunt Clara managed to snare the banker and his largess, the milkman was dropped flat.

Aunt Clara's pride in her resourcefulness, lending a positive glow to her face for the moment, would have turned into snarling contempt had she been able to see the doglike posture of Uncle Ed as he groveled and clawed among the empties for a full bottle, so great was her scorn for the stuff and its users. I had had personal experience of her vehemence on that subject. Before Lena had taken to hanging around with Latham, I used to call on her. Aunt Clara saw me as a likely catch and invited me often to dinner. The affair was getting serious. One Saturday night I went with some other fellows for an excursion on the river. I got liquored up and began to monkey around with the two daughters of the bartender. The three of us promenaded the upper deck arm in arm, singing drunken ballads. Suddenly a lurch threw the lot of us backward into the lap of a seated woman who proved to be Aunt Clara, sitting with a gentleman I didn't recognize. I got no more dinner invitations and was barred from the premises. Then I was gone for a while visiting relatives in another town. When I came back there was talk around town about Lena's bizarre behavior. One day on Main Street in full view of everybody she started tearing off her clothes and flopped all over the sidewalk before collapsing in an hysterical spasm. Neighbors had to help the poor girl get home.

As Mabry arrived home he was relieved to find the yard deserted, as he wanted no witnesses when he dug up his father's money. It offered a balm to his fever. Still, he hesitated in the bushes, a caution duly advised by the memory of his father's violent punishments. Within the month he had felt the sting of the whip. It was the job of Mabry and the hired boy to salt the cows and in general to look after the livestock. Through their negligence two of the animals got loose in the yard, and one of these ran off and was lost. The boys were soundly flogged, then sent to fill the saltboxes in the pasture. Smarting from the lash, Mabry took it into his head to pour a layer of salt over a fresh pile of steaming manure in the yard, covering it perfectly, like white frosting on a cake. The two boys hid behind the trough and waited. Uncle Ed, checking to see if his orders were being carried out, spotted the white mound and went to investigate. Coming near enough to see that the boys had spilled what appeared to be an expensive amount of salt on the ground, he went to the barn and returned with a sack. Muttering "those wasteful boys," he bent to collect the salt, thrusting both hands deep into the pile. When at last he caught up with the fleeing pranksters he beat them nearly unconscious.

I fished with Mabry too," said the plumber. "Pleasant fellow, but just simply worthless. We had a party on the river, a bunch of us men batching it. Drank moonshine and played cards for a couple of days. We took turns fetching the whiskey from a wooden vat hidden in the bushes. When Mabry went to fill the jug he found a fat old sow up on her hind legs drinking out of the vat. Her whole snout and face were down in it. Mabry had just gotten two false teeth to replace the ones his father knocked out. Well sir, he ran to the river and puked those new teeth into the water. Lost 'em. Talley was out there with us too. His wife had kicked him out of the house for a while. He'd gone to the city on business and visited a whorehouse for good measure. Back home screwing his wife, with her just lying there dead still the whole time, he asked her to wiggle some. She said, 'Now I know where you've been!' and threw him out. Made him suffer for it."

I n the barn Uncle Ed finally held in his hand the object of his search, a pint bottle holding perhaps two swallows of clear liquid, found after desperate burrowing under a pile of kindling. As he raised the bottle to his mouth he paused in contemplation of the image of his own father, who on a hunt had raised a jug to the full moon, killed the contents, then cast the empty jug into the weeds, never to take another drink. "You don't have the guts to quit," were his words to Uncle Ed.

In the house Aunt Clara tried to reconstruct the scene of her getaway, to determine whether anyone could have seen her leaving the bank, and whether the banker had been injured or perhaps even knocked unconscious and discovered in his shorts. Fearful of being connected in any way with the affair, she decided to wait until later in the day to go innocently to town to make her inquiries.

Lena's inquiry had already begun. Seeing Latham return and

enter the garage, she followed him inside. "I've come for my an-swer," she said. "What answer?" responded Latham. Upon being informed that she wanted to know whether he was going to marry her, Latham answered "No." Hardly had the words left his lips when Lena pulled the pistol from her bag and fired two shots into his body. Latham slumped to the floor. Lena turned and left, leav-ing the door open behind her, and walked unhurriedly toward home. In the yard she walked past Mabry, who was digging franti-cally with a stick next to a stump. He looked up for an instant into the unseeing blankness of her features, then resumed digging the fourth hole he had tried.

Lena went into the barn. She walked in on Uncle Ed as he licked the final drops from the lip of the bottle. She spoke. "I shot Latham. I saw Clara buck naked in the bank with Mr. Barrett. Mabry is digging up your money." Uncle Ed asked her to repeat what she had said and she did. Jolted from his stupor he snatched the pistol still in her hand and ran outside. He fired a shot that buried itself in the stump after grazing Mabry on the temple, pros-trating him for the moment. At the report Aunt Clara ran out on the veranda. Seeing Uncle Ed with the gun she ran shrieking back inside the house, with Uncle Ed in lumbering pursuit. They chased through the rooms, he shouting abominations at every turn and finally firing at her a single shot. She fell. He ran back outside but Mabry was nowhere in sight. Finding the empty holes and his money gone, Uncle Ed sat down on the stump and put the pis-tol to his head. It discharged against his skull. Lena stood still at the door of the barn, and was there waiting when the sheriff and neighbors arrived, drawn by the shots.

For a long time the plumber didn't say anything. Then he put his roll of tobacco in a pocket in his stained trousers, said "I guess I didn't hear it that way," and traipsed out to the mulberry grove. Who cares what way he heard it. People around here will tell you anything even if they don't know what the hell they're talking about. I guess he thinks he knows something, but he's full of it. He's not even related to any of them. And none of this ever came out in court, because there wasn't a trial. Latham recovered and Lena went to the madhouse, so no suit came of the shooting. Aunt Clara, revived from her fainting spell, shed no light on the cause of Uncle Ed's attack on her, other than to tearfully suggest that such outbursts are common among those who partake of the devil's brew. The small-caliber bullet only scratched Uncle Ed's sodden cranium, its ricochet leaving no more than a flesh wound and a legacy of morose days. Mabry did not return to these parts, settling further west, though likely nothing would have been done to him, for the accused surgeon produced the best citizens to buttress his alibi, and charges were never preferred in the case. The sole fatality was the banker, who was much shaken by the affair, and whom it pleased Providence to carry off by a hemorrhoidal colic. Aunt Clara's grief was muted by the soothing though less remunerative attentions of the local embalmer. As for Gaines, he put on a little weight and said he'd never felt better in his life. And that the "Inhuman Operation" performed on him that the newspapers were full of had in no way interfered in his dealings with the women. I do not doubt him.

Black Pop's O.G.*

FROWN YOU HOSTILE
SMILE YOU A TOM
LOOK TIRED YOU ON JUNK
STUMBLE YOU DRUNK
IF I WASH IM A PIMP
IF I DONT IM A BUM
AND THESE FEET WELL
THESE FEET WONT LET ME BE
NO JUST DONT MAKE NO SENSE
THE WAY MY CORNS ARE HURTING ME

From Melvin Van Peebles, "Just Dont Make No Sense"

One afternoon in early January '94, I sat in a theater located somewhere off of Eighth Avenue, and watched a staged reading of a new musical written by the *singular* Melvin Van Peebles. Some months before, my wife Joy and I had attended a screening at the TriBeCa Film Center of *Vroom Vroom*, a short film Melvin produced and directed for late-night German television, which would later be included in a trilogy of erotic shorts by distinguished directors for the Cannes Film Festival. *Vroom Vroom* is the first American film I know of to present unadulterated black erotic folklore. The only genre of films I can compare it to is the animated "Lemon-Cream" erotic shorts produced in Japan.

---

* Original Guerrilla

Its simple story concerns a virginal rustic derided by his Pops for his (ain't had no) pussy bumps and rejected by the booty-shakin', big-legged gals at a neighborhood barbecue. No matter how hard he tries, m'man can't get hisself any. As m'boys used to say back in the day, "He ain't had pussy since pussy had him!"

Strolling along a back road, our hero saves a local hoodoo woman from getting squashed by a truck. She grants him a wish. He wants two. They huddle in negotiation. The hoodoo woman compromises. And our hero ends up with a motorcycle that morphs into a woman.

If Melvin's new musical blackened the Great White Way anything like his first, *Ain't Supposed to Die a Natural Death*, it promised to be an adventure. I looked forward to the reading, expecting a rousing time, complete with Big Bird on crack. But, due to a prior meeting, I arrived late. I entered the theater, sat down and, to my bafflement, found a stage *loaded with whyte people reciting some Brit-accented, la-di-da, Annie of Green Gables, Anglophile* PBS *bullshit*!!!

Either Melvin had lost his fucking mind or my black ass was in the wrong theater!

As it turned out, the man who had produced such subversive and wholly outrageous works as the album *Brer Soul*, the rated-X-by-an-all-whyte-jury movie *Sweet Sweetback's Baadasssss Song (or Another Mother's Come to Collect Some Dues)* (1971), and the novel *The True American*—as well as conquering Wall Street and siring *New Jack City* director Mario Van Peebles—had written a musical adaptation of *Vanity Fair* (?!?!?!?!) entitled *Becky*.

To my own surprise, not being an Anglophile, I found the experience extremely enjoyable, and thought the musical would prove an enlightening treat for Broadway theatergoers.

At the time of the following interview, which took place in Melvin's Hell's Kitchen co-op apartment, Melvin was preparing for an upcoming film production on the Black Panther Party. He is to co-produce the film with his son, Mario, who will also direct, and Preston Holmes.

DARIUS JAMES: So you came out of Chicago with aspirations of being a writer or a filmmaker?

MELVIN VAN PEEBLES: Oh, no, no, no, no, no! I came out of Chicago with aspirations of getting away. Just to get away from

Van Peebles in *Sweet Sweetback's Baadasssss Song*

home. The schools I came out of you didn't graduate out of. You just had to be big enough to climb over the walls. I just left home and went to college. I didn't know sophisticated things like SAT's or this, that, and the other. Nobody in my family ever went to college. I didn't know that these cats passing out these tests were going to be giving me scores and stuff. (*Laughs.*)

There was this nice guy who talked to me once when I was in college. I was having financial trouble, you know? I had a partial scholarship and I mopped floors and things like that. This guy gave me seventy–five dollars a month just to study. That was great! Except when I got out of college, he said: "Okay, now you're in the Air Force!" I was in the ROTC! It was peacetime and I didn't think there would be any more trouble.

I was out of college thirteen days before I went into the Air Force. When I was twenty, I was already an officer. I didn't have to stay in long, just eighteen months, but they kept me three and a half years. I learned everything the hard way.

DJ: Did you learn photographic and motion-picture skills in the Air Force?

MVP: No, nothing like that. I was the radar operator, bombardier, and navigator on a jet bomber. You see *Dr. Strangelove*?

DJ: Yeah.

MVP: That's what I used to do. I lived in Mexico for a while, where I was a portrait painter, after I got out of the service. Then one day I got tired of being inside. I came back to the States. Even though I had a high specialty, the airlines wouldn't allow minorities into the cockpit, so I ended up doing your basic old manual labor driving cable cars in San Francisco. That would be about 1957—I was twenty–five or twenty–six. People riding the cable car would get on saying [*he speaks in the voice of a castrato Mickey Mouse*], "Ooh! Oooh! Look at this! Isn't this wonderful! I wish I knew more about this!" So I thought, *hmmmm. . . .* And I wrote an article and the article grew. I had some pictures taken and I put it all into a book and I published the book.

One day somebody got on the cable car and said, "Oh, this is a marvelous book. How did you do this?"

"Well, I put some biography here and a photograph there. . . ."

"Oh!" she said, "it's just like a film. You're a director!"

"Is that what it is?" *Hmmmm . . .* so I made a movie. I made my first movie in '57.

DJ: What was it called?

MVP: There were three of them—all shorts which I thought were features. Each one turned out to be eleven minutes long. I was trying to do features. I knew nothing. *Nothing!* You can't even understand how *nothing* nothing is! When I said to this guy I knew who owned a camera that I wanted to make a film, the cat said, you want to make it in 16 or 35?"

"What's that?"

"Millimeter."

"Which is better?"

"Well, 35 is more professional, but my camera is a 16 mm."

"So, how long is a feature?" I had been going to triple features all my life.

"About ninety minutes."

So I figured I could make a feature for $500. That was the cost of ninety minutes of film. I didn't know anything about shooting a film ratio of 20 to 1 or 10 to 1 or none of that shit. Then I forgot you had to develop film. And I didn't know you needed a work print. All I can say is that after I did one thing he would say, "Well, aren't you going to put sound on it?" And I would go, "Oh, shit!" That's all I could say.

When I finished those films, I took them down to Hollywood. I asked every studio for a job. They said, "Yeah, we can offer you a job."

"Really?"

"As an elevator operator."

"What do you mean? I want to *direct*."

"Well, we'll get you a job dancing."

"*Dancing?* What the fuck do I want with *dancing*?!"

At that juncture, I went back to my second love, astronomy. I had been a celestial navigator along with my radar and physics and astronomy and all that crap I had learned in the service. And I moved to Holland to study for my Ph.D. in astronomy.

On my way there, I had these three short films I'd made under my arm. I came here to New York to catch the boat because I couldn't afford a plane. Some guy took the films on rental and happened to show them in France. And they said, "Jesus, this man's a genius! Where is he? He should be making films!" The Cinémathèque wrote me a nice postcard in Amsterdam saying, "What are you doing? You should be making films!"

So I went to France. And the day I arrived, the Cinémathèque rolled out the red carpet. They took me to a screening room, showed my films. We came downstairs. It was about nine o'clock at night. It was dark. "It's wonderful! You're a genius!" Everybody kissed me on both cheeks and drove off down the Champs Elysées. They left me with three cans of film, two wet cheeks, and not a fuckin' penny in my pocket.

DJ: That's when you got a job translating *Mad* magazine into French.

MVP: I had to learn how to speak French first.

DJ: But weren't you initially writing in French?

MVP: Initially, I was begging. I couldn't play an instrument so I got a kazoo. My big numbers were "La Bamba" and "Take This Hammer." I just hustled my way around Paris. And little by little, I began to know a few people. But I decided very early on that I wouldn't hang with Americans because Americans there were the same as they were here. Later I discovered there's a French law that says a French writer can have a temporary film director's card. So I made myself a French writer. I wrote *A Bear for the F.B.I.* A friend helped me translate it into French and I was trying to get it published.

Then one day I was walking down the street and heard somebody say, "I don't think that's right. . . ." I thought, "Who the hell is saying this?" I looked around and I was alone and I realized I had said it. I had read the headlines of a French newspaper. I didn't know I could read French and all of a sudden I was reading headlines. The story was about a murder and it sounded fishy to me. So I went and talked to the head of this magazine, a sort of French *Newsweek*, and asked him to let me go and investigate. I went out and got a scoop! Almost got murdered, found out this, that, and the other thing. It was like a bad movie. What I had discovered was so important it was used in the transcript of the trial.

After that, the people who'd been throwing me out the door the day before started asking, "Didn't you have a book?" In the meantime an American literary agent looking for American writers who lived in France searched me out and asked me to write a book. He didn't know I was black and when he saw me, he freaked. He said, "Well, we should be able to do business. How about writing me a black book?"

"So what's a black book?"

"They're usually written in the third person." He said I needed to include a certain amount of rage. So I wrote *The True American.* He got pissed off and wouldn't publish it.

Then when I came back to the States in 1967 as one of the French delegates to the San Francisco Film Festival, I was really taken by the fact that there were no protest songs by our folks. It was all Bob Dylan and Joan Baez.

DJ: There's Odetta.

MVP: They're singing the same songs but they weren't writing them the same way. There was Odetta and Richie Havens and so forth. You know what's being said in the music magazines and all this crap about how I invented rap? When I did it, what I wanted to say didn't fit the form. So I said, "What the fuck, I'll do my own form." At the time people didn't know what to call it. "Well, it's spoken poetry." No, no, no, no, no! In fact there's a German term for it—*Sprechstimme.* Each song I had done was a monologue and made up the play *Ain't Supposed to Die a Natural Death,* which did theatrically what *Sweetback* did cinematically. It broke a lot of barriers for us. And also what happened was that the revolutionary message was preempted and became counterrevolutionary*—subliminally counterrevolutionary—without people ever realizing and it was still being hawked as a revolutionary message. Nothing like that had ever happened before. Nelson George did a very interesting article on that in the *Voice.*

DJ: "Buppies, B-boys, Baps and Bohos." Yeah, it was a piece tracing black cultural evolution through the '70s and tying it to the so-called New Black Aesthetic.

MVP: Yeah, being self-taught had its advantages. I didn't really

---

* I.e., *Shaft.*

have any influences. There were no modern American black directors. All I saw in movies were lynchings. I just looked out the window. I took my cue from what I thought was life. Not Truffaut or any of those secondary sources. The reason I did what I did cinematically was because I didn't know what I couldn't do. Physically the bumble bee can't fly but it doesn't know that, so it does, you know. Later I learned the language of Kurosawa and Eisenstein, but that was a different thing. It had nothing to do with my own work. Since it was all new to me, I just did it the way I felt it should be done. Have you ever heard any of my early records?

DJ: They used to play them on WYBC on Sunday afternoons. I saw a section from *Ain't Supposed to Die a Natural Death* presented the weekend you were doing lectures around New Haven. Obviously your satirical imagery was a big influence on me. It had impact. There were a number of people, including yourself, who were working in this radical mode. And it seems to have disappeared.

MVP: That got preempted into the full politicism of the current rap and the almost retro '80s macho attitude. It's now been passed back to the young people.

DJ: In terms of *Sweetback*, I thought what you were able to accomplish filmically was what The Last Poets were able to do orally. *Sweetback* is urban, visual poetry.

MVP: That's why it's called a *Baadasssss Song*. It came out in 1970. My stuff predates The Last Poets and I knew them. They began to use that form and it was great. The music to *Ain't Supposed to Die* predated *Sweetback*. You see, I was always good at guerrilla warfare. I did not have enough money to do theater. I did an album and through the album I sold it as a play. I just did it step by step. Most people don't even know I'm a writer. Most people think of me as a filmmaker. Theater people think of me as a theater man. But I'm primarily just a writer who got tired of getting dissed.

DJ: One of the things that's always impressed me about *Sweetback* was the fact that Huey Newton devoted an entire issue of the Black Panther Party's newspaper to it when it first came out.

MVP: When all the niggas was running for cover, behind walls an' shit, the Panthers were great.

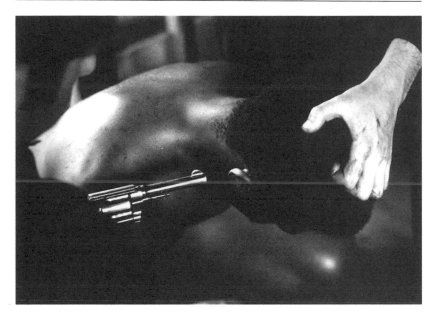

Sweet Sweetback's Baadasssss Song

Melvin leaves and returns with his first album Brer Soul. *He points to a caption on the back that reads, "Free Huey."*

MVP: This was long before *Sweetback.* All the lyrics are printed on the album. I got a phone call one day from a guy working at some bad-boys school here in New York. He said, "We've been trying to teach kids to read and with your album, they're reading because they're interested in what the words say."

Melvin plays the album. Backed by minimalist Charles Mingus–like music, it is "spoken-word performance" at its raw best. No detachable MTV penis here. This is the real shit.

MVP: I didn't know the Panthers or anything else. Everybody was ducking for cover, and those people who had a chance to say something weren't saying it, and I didn't give a shit. They said I was going to lose sales, but what's it all about, Alfie? You know what I mean? I'm saying what needs to be done.

DJ: You present a particular kind of message that is consistently co-opted and switched. Do you want to talk about that?

MVP: I think it was great marketing strategy. I don't think much of this happens on a conscious level. And the golden rule is that he who has the gold makes the rules. I had a three-picture deal with Columbia Pictures, after *Watermelon Man*, but I wanted to say what I wanted to say. They wouldn't do *Sweetback* and I realized I needed another studio to produce this movie. So, one day, I looked in the mirror, shaving, and I said, "Melvin, this is your studio."

DJ: Over the years, how have you struggled with the problem of mainstreaming your work? Bleaching it out?

MVP: I don't have any problem with that: *I can't do it!*

An
Actor's Life

THE BABY DAUGHTER YOU DESERTED HAS GROWN UP TO BE A TV STAR.

OUR DEATH·MASKS MELTING IN A KISS,
HER LIPS SMEARED ALL OVER HER FACE.
HER KISS IS CATCHING, I'M CATCHING MY DEATH-KISS.
HER PERFUME CLEARED THE AIR OF CIGARETTE SMOKE.
HER FILTER TIP SMEARED WITH LIPSTICK TRACES.
HER NOSE LOADED WITH POWDER TO BLOW.
READ SMEARED RED ALL OVER THE PAGE.
HER RED SMEAR WRAPPED IN STARS N'STRIPES.
THE GLANS LENS FILTER SKINNED ROSE RED.
HER HEAD RAISING THE DEAD.

A DAY IN SOMINEX TOWN, A DAY LIKE ANY OTHER.
THE NEIGBORHOOD OF CARBON MONOXIDE.

USING DAD'S OLDS.

STEREO DYIN'.

A THINNING OF THE RANKS.

STONERS FELL LIKE DOMINOS.

BRO'S LIKE THAT.

A FAINT SMELL OF BURNING HEMP MIXED IN.

THERE IS NO AIR TO BREATHE ON—IN YOUR ANAHEIM.

MORE THAN EVER HE WANTED TO DIE.

KRYPTONITE KISSES.

THIS CHILLY CARESS MIGHT HAVE COME FROM THE WING OF A BAT.

I turned my father in to HUAC.

LITTLE OR NO PLOT.

A SENSELESS KILLING.

An Actor's Life

Raymond Pettibon's drawings recall the cheap allure of film noir and pulp fiction, but also signal a loss of faith in popular culture as a wellspring for art. From the vantage point of a mythic City Of Angels reverberating within the chaos of Mike Davis's *City Of Quartz*, Pettibon deflates the "utopian" irony that once surrounded Pop Art and its '80s kin. There along the fault-line of impending millennial disintegration, Pettibon plumbs the trashier precincts of Hollywood, divining the roots of a culture that consumes itself while reveling in its indifference to the violence around it.

This kind of pervasive alienation is central to the aesthetics of film noir, which is why its permutations in television, comics, literature, and politics form a touchstone for Pettibon's work. His neurasthenic posture, however, strips noir of its romantic anti-heroism and emphasizes instead the paranoia implicit in its dark glamour. As in one drawing that reads "Little Or No Plot, A Senseless Killing," Pettibon fears where America is heading because he knows where it's coming from.

Thus Pettibon makes reference to classic noir practitioners like Bob Kane (the creator of *Batman* comics) but belies the original's night-prowling authority. When Batman appears, he is a literal and somewhat flabby shadow of his former self: an all-too plausible amalgam of concerned parent and predatory chickenhawk trolling for his erstwhile charge in an alley straight out of a Rod Serling cliché. Coming upon Robin in homoerotic flagrante, Pettibon's Caped Crusader is confronted by the hypocrisy of his own sexual mores as the texts reads, "I'll stonewall your ass, you fairy fag-basher. . . .Yeah, like we don't know about you and your Boy Wonder . . . ward? And you're Ward Cleaver."

Pettibon's channel surfing and Joycean punning represent the disjointedness that is the American dreamlife. But there is also a poignancy that suffuses his otherwise hard-boiled writing, a voice that is collective in nature. Pettibon's texts are written from the margin, the internalized dialogue of the truly dispossessed. In this manner, he regurgitates chunks of the media as a form of reclamation, taking back the lives reduced to fiction by the confessional maw of Geraldo, Phil, and Oprah.

Pettibon recognizes that Pop Art's irony, originally meant to forestall an insatiable media culture, was long ago consumed by it. What's left is a situation in which feeling has become a commodity to be inflated or wrung dry at will. Pettibon's America is a reality distorted by television, but in a manner far different from that intended by corporate demographers. "The Baby Daughter You Deserted Has Grown Up To Be A TV Star," reads another drawing's caption, placed above a featureless male figure sitting cross-legged on a bed. In the generic desolation of a motel room or trailer park, his existence has been pared down to the TV set in front of him. In a less exhausted time, Pettibon seems to suggest, this image might have been viewed as ironic, but not now.

—Howard Halle

The World is Round

Freedom begins with a double cordon of cops and a door with thick bars, behind which they lock us all up. *Flüchtlingslager Traiskirchen bei Wien.* Suddenly we are all *Flüchtlinge,* refugees. *Nummer. Name. Passport.* Trochees. *Tschechoslowakei.* Not very cleverly, I wipe the fingerprint ink all over my face with my hands. Czechs, Poles, Hungarians, Iranians. Finally we are all registered. To which country do we wish to go? We all have to see the doctor for an examination. Form an orderly line in front of the office door. One line for men, one line for women, children stay with your mothers. Does everyone here understand Polish? The Afghani interpreter will be here next Thursday. *Deutsch? Verstehen? Do you understand? Nichts?* Does everyone here understand Polish? Each of you has the right to medical treatment free of charge. You must tell us now whether you have had any of the following illnesses: viral hepatitis, gonorrhea, syphilis. . . . Whoever requires it will receive medical attention. Does everyone here understand Polish? Anyone who is ill, please step out of the line.

The isolation ward is a long corridor on the third floor of the building. A row of green doors opening into the rooms. Apparently, the camp had once been a military garrison. Now it is ours. But it still smells of the army: greasy mess tins, coarse camp soap, the menthol toothpaste that we are also issued, the horse blankets that slip from between our hands. *Zimmer achtundneunzig*, says the Austrian. *Schlafen.* You will sleep there. *Verstehen?*

Two million languages, sweat, bustle, and children crying. Windows without bars open out onto the courtyard, conveying the last trembling scents of linden blossoms. Smell is the only sense I am able to employ in the slightest. Several pairs of curious eyes peer out the open door of the room. You're new. Where from? What language do you speak? Where is it you want to go, what do you want, what sort of person are you? But none of that is important. The main thing, my dear girl, is that you don't steal.

•　•　•

I crawl into the top bunk by the window and form a nest from the two sheets and military blanket. The sheets are fresh, laundered, enormously clean-smelling. I concentrate on making my bed. Sleep is indispensable and extremely important. In a minute I know the names of the others and where they are headed. Now we are all refugees. The room smells of wet plaster, a flaking canvas painted by moisture seeping down from the upper corners: we are on the top floor, it probably leaks in from the roof. The water has decorated the ceiling and top halves of the walls with golden maps. The charts according to which Columbus guided his boats. Maps of lands, seas, and oceans. Maps of the continents that we will someday reach.

•　•　•

And, of course, the dream returns the instant I am without a man, a dream borne from a childhood so distant that it brings back the pain of sprouting wings. A dream from the illustrated book of Saint-Exupéry; a dream in which you touch and smell and live with your very own self—and at the same time you see yourself as a tiny orange fleck on a blue planet, beyond which sets a violet star.

•　•　•

At five-thirty in the morning an Austrian cop bangs on the door: "Breakfast! Brea-a-akfaaast! *Essen! Essen!*" The two gay Hungarian girls on the bunk below me come untwined and start blabbering. Or at least the Czech who keeps endlessly reminding us that he is the head of a family calls it blabbering because he cannot understand it. We have no language in common with the Hungarian girls.

And so from the very first days, we are divided into *us* and *them*. We are the Czechs. The Slovaks, to a lesser degree. The Poles, marginally. We are *us* inasmuch as we can understand one another, even though the most important thing is that I am myself. All the others, of course, are riffraff.

"*Essen!*" The cop pounds on the door and throws it wide open. One of us gets up, rubs the sleep from his eyes, and goes for rolls and weak coffee. The coffee goes into an enormous water can that has to last all day.

The corridor comes alive with bustle. A couple of hungry souls go dashing off to breakfast. The low sun already gilds stripes of dust in the corridor. A stripe creeps from each window. Families scold their children and hunt for them in the corridor. An Afghan woman breaks pieces off a roll. She has on a sari with a veil up to her nose, and she keeps turning away, toward the wall, in order to stick another little chunk into her mouth beneath the veil. From behind the veil peer her exhausted chestnut eyes. I try English on her. She doesn't understand—or is she just not reacting? Perhaps they too have divided everyone into *us* and *them*? I want to know. But there is no one to ask. Even though, of course, everyone knows everything.

I play dice with some Poles. Tadeusz makes the dice out of pieces of bread: he rolls them for a long time between his fingers, spitting in his palms, then flattens the sides on the edge of the table and uses a match to impress into them the one two three four five six. Then he dries them in the sun that slants beneath the window. Tadek always knows what to do with himself: he has learned this in prison. He was one of the first members of Solidarity. That sounds interesting. I sleep with him. Tadek has a wife and two children at home. He is headed to Canada, they will come after him. He will have to work hard in order to pay their way from Poland. But hopefully in a couple of years. . . .

"Doesn't it bother you to be unfaithful?"
"Not at all. Does it bother you?"
"I've got no one to be faithful to."
"At least there's no one for you to miss."
(No one to miss. No one to miss, Standa?)

● ● ●

In the dream a stark-naked fool steps on the Earth and it spins like a centrifuge, with dizzying speed, dizzying, more and more dizzying. I press myself against Tadek. I don't want to see the fool smash his face in.

● ● ●

Breakfast, *essen, essen,* a couple of unfinished sentences, euphoria, joylessness, and fear. Why are we stuck here? Because we are waiting for a hearing. A hearing? Yes, from the Austrians, sure, they call you for your hearing after all this has driven you nuts, but before anybody tells you what you should say to them. They ask you what country you want to go to and what reasons you had for leaving. Reasons? Reasons, of course, after all it's basically a request for asylum. Asylum . . . sure. In those papers they gave you to sign there's also an application for Austrian asylum. You can't stay in Austria without it.

Noon, chow time, pink meal tickets and a line in the mess hall, where Middle Eastern–looking cutthroats throw everything in a mess tin and cover it with gravy. Food is enormously important, because it helps a person think. Eat a lot of fish. It's good for you, they say. Perhaps the poor things died for our sake. We chow down in the mess hall, choking on the bones. How can they possibly serve carp in gravy, the Czechs fume. Now, now, young man, this isn't home, is it? You're in the sticks now. We dig away with our spoons, seated around rickety tables. We are not allowed to take food upstairs. We would be feeding the roaches. And they are fat enough already.

● ● ●

The stark-naked fool attempts to drag a bunch of balloons across a Nevada desert filled with cacti. The balloons break and are as pained as pierced souls. The cacti grow together into an impenetrable wall, gray, tall, and senseless, which from now on separates me and Standa. And white, hot bodies try to press through the barbed wire. While from their stabbing wounds, lacerations, and gunshot wounds pour streams of green despair.

Smells, dust, longing, filth, and euphoria. Why are there so many of us on this earth? It is crammed full of people with the same destiny, stepping on one another, fighting, shouting one another down, each one desperately alone.

•   •   •

EVERY FRIDAY BETWEEN EIGHT AND NINE IN THE MORNING, IT IS NECESSARY FOR EVERY REFUGEE TO TAKE A BATH, declares the announcement written in seven languages on the wall of the isolation ward. Some of us need it. A trip under escort across the yard. One line for men, one line for women, children stay with your mothers. A mass of stenches, steam, children yelling. The overwhelming, omnipresent smell of coarse soap. An Afghan woman raising her sari and bathing her ankles under the shower. Children of every color and type splashing one another. Hygiene is enormously important. Because it helps a person not to be a pig.

It is noon on Friday, and those of us who do not have their own soap smell of the officially issued camp soap. Menthol toothpaste wafts from many a mouth. There are an awful lot of us here: us, the uprooted ones.

•   •   •

Tadeusz is writing a letter to his wife. One more for the pile that will never be sent. I take the ballpoint pen from his hand and kiss him: Teach me some Polish! We are playing dice with the other Poles. Someone has smuggled in a bottle of Wodka Wyborowa. The sun lurches drunkenly through our cell. I am writing a letter to Standa, one I will never send. In it I am faithful to him. Total bullshit. Different rules apply here and now, the rules of contact and new acquaintance, the rule of grab whatever you can, the rule that it is good to drive away the dream. The rule that we need one another, because otherwise we are all alone in this big, wide world.

•   •   •

There are a million things I don't understand. In the isolation ward I am learning the camp like a foreign language: slowly, falteringly, without a textbook. And it is so damned easy to get things wrong.

•   •   •

Beneath the windows of the isolation ward stand those who have been released a few days ago into the free camp, craning their necks and shouting up at us. By means of strings we lower down to them they send up chocolate and cigarettes and Wodka Wyborowa. The camp below smells of freedom. The scent of linden is almost entirely gone by now.

•   •   •

And when the lights go out in the evening, the glow of Vienna's lights beyond the window illuminates the water paintings on the plaster ceiling. Those golden brown outlines that—if you forget almost everything you know about geography—remind you of the continents.

Europe.

Asia.

America.

With half-closed eyes I fashion their shapes above me. They are mixed together, confused, just like we are. They are thrown around like cards on a table. Pick a card, any card, don't hesitate, any card at all. Will it be the ace of hearts or the old maid? Any card at all. Any card. Don't hesitate. No *time* to think it over. And you must take a card!

•   •   •

Sleep is enormously important, because you don't have to think. About the continents on the ceiling. About Europe. Or America. The Hungarian girls below me are at it again. The Czech clicks his tongue: Tsk! Tsk! And since my bunk is connected to theirs, the tall metal bars convey to me the tremblings of their heavenly love and their tender Hungarian blabberings. I already know why this bunk has been left for me.

But I also know that I don't actually want to sleep, that the dream is lurking just behind my eyelids: that it will be here immediately, the instant I take my eyes off my continents. My continents, to which I long to travel.

Europe, Asia, America, Africa, Australia, Antarctica. I gaze at my continents. They might just as easily be clouds, or irises. What if I thought about irises? Anything would be better than that dream.

• • •

America.
Canada.
Australia.

Pick a country to apply to. Supposedly no one else would take you. You could also stay in Europe, but that doesn't pay these days. You say you need information? You say you need time? Well, forget about it, you're buying a pig in a poke. For that matter, why didn't you know before you took off just where you were headed? Did you think that everyone here was waiting around to take care of you? Did you think that everyone here loved you?

Didn't you realize that the world existed before you came?

• • •

—So, young man, you've got an uncle in Australia and he wants you there, well, whaddya know. By all means, go there, but watch out! These uncles aren't always just dependable old milkcows, mark my words, these uncles are liable to bleed you dry, my dear boy. Haven't you heard about the Czech guy in America who worked for his darling uncle for a dollar fifty an hour—for eleven years?! A dollar fifty an hour! The average hourly wage in the States is

twenty-two dollars and thirty-seven cents, so just watch out, make
sure they give you more.

—But that was in America. . . .

—Sure, that was in America, but the same thing can happen
to you in Australia, young man, do you really have to—

—The hourly wage there is not twenty-two dollars! My aunt
wrote me that it's more like five!

—Well, I don't know where your dear old aunt got her—

—I heard it's eighteen.

—You see that, eighteen or twenty-two. If you're working for
less, you're getting exploited, mark my words.

—You'll get exploited no matter what.

—I heard that in Canada—

—Forget about Canada! They won't take an unmarried man,
don't you know that? Nothing but families with children, if that.

—But didn't they accept that locksmith? My husband says—

—Sure, a locksmith, young lady, a locksmith, maybe. But an
unmarried *intellectual* they would never take. Besides, you can easily wait more than a year for Canada. They've got good security,
social security, understand, so they're scared people will go over
there to, say, study or something. Living on that security. You can
kiss your Canada goodbye. They've got security over there.

—Supposedly it's even better in Sweden.

—Yes, it's better there, young man, plus they've got cute little
whores and dirty Swedish movies, but as soon as you get there they
sign you up for Swedish classes, and if you can't get that gibberish
into your thick skull, they lock you up.

—That's ridiculous—

—Lock you up, I tell you, they used to cut your hand off for
stealing over there. And if you—

—The Swedes haven't been taking anyone for a long time.

—Sure, I'm telling you, they already have a load of émigrés.
And those Swedes don't like foreigners much. You'll be an immi-
grant till the day you die.

—That's what we'd be here, too.

—That's what you'll be everywhere—and they'll never let you
forget it, either. Here in Austria, for example—

—Supposedly it's even worse in Switzerland!

—Oh, sure, in Switzerland! You'll never get to Switzerland,

young man, even if you cut yourself up into little pieces and mail yourself there. Supposedly they want to maintain the purity of the population, goddamn yodelers. You haven't heard about the guy who lived there peacefully for *five years*, they kept promising him asylum, then, finally, after five years, they sent him off to Prague in handcuffs? The Swiss will—

—They did the same thing to some Poles!

—What they did to our Polish brothers over there doesn't interest me one bit, let them do whatever they want with the Polacks, we're already up to our ears in them here and the whole place stinks of piss. They're doing this to *us*, to Czechs, understand! The minute you set foot in Switzerland you'll never be sure what will happen, till the day you die! And listening to those damned bells of theirs, and all their sacred cows! Don't you know anything: even once you've got asylum it takes twelve years before they'll give you Swiss citizenship. Twelve goddamn years! . . .

• • •

I stagger out of the stifling room like a phantom and go to get some fresh air in the corridor, which smells of summer and lindens just past blossoming. . . .

I am playing dice with the Pole, Tadeusz. He smiles at me over the table, strokes my hand—and his eyes, with their look of solidarity, of Solidarity, *Solidarność*, wink at me from the cloud of smoke pluming from his densely packed *papierosa*. He teaches me the Polish for "book" and "I like you very much" and "It doesn't matter." "Are you coming over tonight?" I nod and go to shower. There is even a shower in the bathroom, but the faucet on it doesn't work. I wash my body with a long hose connected to the sink tap, previously installed by someone for this purpose. I step in the suds, the smell of laundry soap; I step in the filth from other female bodies, preparing myself to be touched. I wash my underarms, my back, my throat; I splash around, happy as a seal pup. I wash my crotch in the stream of water, and the water voluptuously suggests everything I have planned for that night. In the line of those also longing to wash, two Czech mothers lean together. They watch me sloshing happily, their eyes revealing certain suspicion. One whispers something to the other. I sleep around, they say. So be it.

Then I go to Tadek's, take the ballpoint pen he is again using to put together a letter to his wife. "I'm lonely, Tadek. But I see some new people have moved into your room . . . with kids. . . ."

"It doesn't matter. *To nie przeszkadza.*"

Tadek and I sit on his bed, and several newly arrived Polish parents observe us reproachfully. What are these two going to do? Right here in front of the children? As soon as the lights go out I forget everything. I get undressed quickly beside him under the blanket.

The smell of soap, shaving cream, and a strong Polish *papierosa.* Each man smells differently. Each one has a slightly different taste, too, and each one has a different way of chasing the dream away. Nevertheless, each of them chases it away. I open myself to Tadek in the dark. I know that today we have to be quiet, there are children here, there can't be even the slightest squeak of the bed, and this fact transforms longing into passion and passion into ecstasy. It seems to us that we love each other.

•　•　•

Breakfast. Coffee. Dice with Tadeusz. He tells me about Solidarity. It sounds like a Russian fable about the Revolution. When will he give it a rest, this Tadeusz, as if the whole world were nothing but *Solidarność.* He carves an indecent portrait of Jaruzelski into the table. Another act of resistance, I think. Lunch. Pink meal tickets. Blue and white meal tickets, too. The white ones are for Muslims and the blue for nursing mothers. Gradually I am beginning to perceive the things around me. First, I see colors. The colors of faces, hair, clothes, meal tickets. The Austrian cook punches the meal tickets with a hole punch. Pink, white, and blue confetti rains onto the mess-hall floor like an illusion of colored wind. A tanned individual dumps an undercooked slice of leg roast into your tin. They have good stuff to cook with, but they don't know what they're doing. Or else they are saving the best for themselves.

•　•　•

A couple of unfinished conversations. Dice with Tadeusz. "Dinner! *Essen!*" Pink meal tickets and a hunk of Hungarian sausage. Salad of sliced Chinese cabbage, only slightly rotten, a source of vitamin C. We live like cabbage, greenly, vegetatively. The earth is green, blue, and orange. Mostly blue. Like a tangerine.

● ● ●

Why did you leave? Did you have reasons? Reasons? Right, *political* ones, good sound political reasons? Were you oppressed in your homeland? What resistance groups did you belong to? What do you have to show for yourself, hero? Do you have any scars, bullet wounds, burns, marks on your body, an eye patch? Did you have reasons for leaving, hero? Then name them for me: one two three four. You say you've never thought about it before? Well, it's time you started, hero, because the Austrians will be asking you about it pretty damned soon at your hearing.

—Why did you run away?

—Now see here, take my advice and don't go around asking people about that. These Austrians'll be asking you about that plenty, until you're soft in the head, at all those hearings. Besides, I have nothing to fear. We, dear boy, were dissidents, and I'm going to shout it out right in their faces: Sirs, we were dissidents— and I—

—But real dissidents don't have to go through the camps at all. They get asylum right in Vienna.

—Oh sure, you're talking about the Charterists! Those Charterists, as soon as they get here they have everything all set up for them by their comrades who got here before them. Apartments and social security and German courses—and asylum, young man, within three days, so they can start lounging around on that social security and bullshitting right away. They're all just a bunch of thieves.

—Charterists? The ones who signed the Charter '77? You dare to call them thieves? They were the only ones in Czechoslovakia who stood for anything—don't you know how they were hounded? Thrown out of work, school, locked up, how the state made problems for their *children*, even kids in grade school. And you call them thieves?

—Well, apparently you are not a Charterist, inasmuch as you'd be sitting in your pretty little nest in Mother Vienna. So why do

you defend them? Go to Vienna to see them for yourself. A gang
of scum, they are, all of them.

—I think the ones who stayed are the real heroes.

—Well, the ones who stayed, maybe, but the ones who come
here are a bunch of scum! They were cruel to them, you say? Bull!
They sweated through a couple of interrogations, and when they
applied to emigrate they let them go in a year.

—But that year—

—That year did them no harm. Do you think they didn't have
it all planned out? And then they come here straight into the lap
of luxury, a nice little apartment with all the conveniences, collecting all sorts of aid. How long are these Austrian bastards going to
suck us dry before we get what their darling Charterists get right
out of the gate? All I'd give them is a good flogging—

—And just what sort of dissident are *you*?

—Me, young man, me? I was *imprisoned* over there, I sat biting
my nails for over five years in a criminal institution, wrongly con-
victed for political reasons! But when those chestnuts call me in
for my interview, I'm going to tell them straight out: Sirs, I—

—Olda, you went to jail for that short delivery.

—Quiet, you! Stupid woman! You don't know what you're talking about! I was a political prisoner and no one can say otherwise!
I was a victim of the regime! And that's exactly what I'll tell them,
too, I'll get it through their thick skulls. . . .

• • •

Europe. Asia. America.

Africa. Australia. Antarctica.

My heart is an orphaned blue flake of ice. Is Antarctica still
accepting émigrés from Czechoslovakia? Or are they trying to pre-
serve the purity of the population? Sorry, they're only taking polar
bears this year. . . .

Africa. Asia. America.

Stick your head in a kangaroo's pouch and croak. Pink, white,
blue meal tickets. A flood of new fugitives from somewhere, oh,
they are all still so laughably foolish. A million languages. Exhausted Afghani eyes. The reproachful eyes of the couple with
children in Tadek's room. The sole of a shoe instead of dinner,

and cabbage salad. The color of tangerines. Europe. Asia. America. Do you have any relatives there, miss? Tadek and I are playing dice made from bread. He wants me to go with him to Canada. He's in love with me, he says. Idiot.

●   ●   ●

Marks on the body. Scars. Burns.

Why do you want to be here? Why don't you want to be there? Why don't you just go someplace else?

Translated from the Czech by David Powelstock

Linda Nicklin

Even as we sat together
in the very first class
I knew she came from a place
—meaning a warp of culture
some ideal actual space
I'd never actually been near
at least not on this side
of the Irish Sea

and so without desire
with a frugal disinterest
I began to draw a picture
—touching and naïf
of a market town in Lincolnshire
that she didn't want to leave
the draper's shop
where she bought those skirts
that geranium frock
the jackets like school blazers
—two pubs a chapel
a skewed spire
and some brick houses
in each interior
the alum verities of dissent
—starchcolored wallpaper
a view of Mablethorpe
maybe the Authorized Version
—it was dull

it was a bore
no crack
no folklore
and all the while the enormous
flat wheatfields went on
and on . . . I imagined more
and then I didn't
for at 18 you don't want
that awful middle-England stasis
—the Saxon handpainted names
on each glazed shopfront
the hardware the bakery
those empty shimmering
those crazed landscapes
where every road says simply
there's no escape
stay decent stay here
—but she'd caught a bus fifty miles
into the next county
and now I'm unpicking a guilt
about working her name
into a thin realist
irrecoverable timespot
a sort of lifesculpture
—with her definite chin
her boyish hair
that almost parched skin
she could have been
a kind of weekly cousin
whose name rang true
like the milled rim on a coin
as it hithits the counter

Raymond Rohauer interviews Groucho Marx.

Raymond Rohauer: King of the Film Freebooters

If Martin Davis, erstwhile head of Paramount Pictures, or young film-producing tycoon Joel Silver were suddenly to drop dead, there would of course be a certain amount of rejoicing—men in their position make many enemies—and a great deal of jockeying for survival positions among their confederates. But the dust would soon settle, and six months later, apart from immediate family and friends, nobody would remember or care. Certainly not members of the moviegoing public.

But a much less publicized, and apparently smaller, cog in the industry wheel—one Raymond Rohauer—died, in his sixties, on November 10, 1987, and the dust still hasn't settled. Nor has *anyone* who had any contact with him forgotten him. Most people—certainly those who came up against him in business—considered him a film pirate. I prefer the term "freebooter" since it suggests that certain cavalier charm that Rohauer possessed. Pirates were interested only in loot, plunder, and the wealth it brought; Rohauer was far more concerned with the extension of *power* the loot could buy. He was a complex and fascinating character: there was as much of Jack London's Wolf Larsen in his makeup as there was Captain Kidd. In a historical context, he could be likened to the French Vidocq, the thief who became Paris's chief of police, and was played so memorably by George Sanders in Douglas Sirk's

Scandal in Paris (1946). Indeed, if there were any way to turn the manipulation of copyright laws into a visually and dramatically exciting script, then the Rohauer story could have been an even more engrossing film than Robert Altman's *The Player*.

Ironically, considering his major role in bringing dead films and forgotten personalities back to life, Rohauer's early career included a brief stint as a Los Angeles grave digger. He made his first mark in the film business, however, in the late '40s with Hollywood's Coronet Theater, a bizarre combination of art house, film society, and exploitation cinema. Production Code censorship was still at its peak, and by operating as a private film society Rohauer could legally show revivals, European imports, and experimental films that were all forbidden, usually for their sexual content, to normal commercial exhibition. While he posed as a crusading force for artistic expression, however, Rohauer filled his notorious foldout mailing programs with salacious or sensationalist promises that the films themselves (often of genuine merit) failed to supply. The French writer and director Jacques Prévert, invariably, through "typographical error," found his name spelled "Pervert."

Rohauer's passion for acquisition began during this period: everything that passed through the Coronet's projectors somehow found itself copied and added to the permanent Rohauer archives—a source of particular annoyance to the Museum of Modern Art when Rohauer entered the distribution field himself and didn't always bother to remove the logos and very recognizable MoMA forewords from his duped copies. A number of other patterns in Rohauer's career were also established at this time: he bought the rights to many films (especially European films standing no other chance of U.S. release that were thus available quite economically); he established lasting relationships with a number of surviving directors and stars of the silent era (there were many such, shamefully neglected in the Hollywood of the late '40s); and he was largely responsible for rescuing much of the work of Stan Laurel and Buster Keaton. (Many of Keaton's 35mm prints came into Rohauer's hands after the actor James Mason discovered them in the garage of Keaton's former house and notified Rohauer at the Coronet.)

Around this time, Rohauer also began to make the first in a long string of enemies whom he happily combatted through the legal system. And his number one enemy in Hollywood was John Hampton, the director of a theater devoted entirely to silent movies, which showed just enough of a profit to keep it solvent. Hollywood studios generally turned a blind eye to Hampton's commercially harmless copyright violations. Rohauer, on the other hand, devoted an inordinate amount of time to suing Hampton for showing material that Rohauer claimed to own and to spurring others on to do likewise.

Eventually, despite the Coronet's function as a valuable showcase for serious Los Angeles avant garde filmmakers like Kenneth Anger, its sexually immoral reputation got it into serious trouble with the L.A. vice squad. Rohauer might have successfully seen it through, but the theater had already served its purpose in establishing him as an exhibitor and distributor and he was ready to move on—to New York.

As film curator of the Gallery of Modern Art—a short-lived alternative to the Museum of Modern Art funded by millionaire dilettante Huntington Hartford—Rohauer had only a small theater at his disposal, but he made the most of it, bringing in personalities such as British star of the '30s Jessie Matthews, choreographer / director Busby Berkeley, and Berkeley's star Ruby Keeler for well-deserved tributes. But to Rohauer, the main appeal of the job was the name of the venue—the Gallery of Modern Art. It was all too easy to refer to it (accidentally) as the Museum of Modern Art, and to see himself in print as the curator of the *Museum*—while his old enemies at MoMA could only squirm in dismay.

Rohauer's tenure with the Gallery was brief—or to be fair, the Gallery's tenure as an alternate to the Museum was brief. It was too small to be profitable with the expenses incurred by Rohauer's programming. But it gave him his foothold in New York, and from then on he devoted himself solely to his effort to buy, acquire, or control everything in the film world that wasn't tied down. Buster Keaton's films, most of which were already in the public domain (save a few early Metro films Rohauer had managed to acquire through bravado and a good lawyer), were to be the mainstay of Rohauer's operations. At revival festivals in the United States and abroad, initially with Keaton himself as a participant, they brought in real money. Later TV usage of the Keaton material brought further revenue—as did Rohauer's lawsuits against anyone who used so much as a frame or still of Keaton's footage without payment.

Rohauer knew the copyright laws inside and out. And they varied in Europe, to his advantage. He knew that even if a film were in the public domain, it could be based on a story that was not. Very often, *usually*, the author was dead and the descendants had no knowledge of or interest in the property. Rohauer would seek them out, press a hundred dollars or so into their innocent hands, and come away with the story rights. In this way, he was able to sneak Rudolph Valentino's *The Sheik* away from Paramount, and to insert himself as a kind of executive producer into Radley Metzger's 1978 remake of *The Cat and the Canary*. By quietly acquiring the story rights to a J. B. Priestley novel, he was also able to claim exclusive distribution rights to one of Universal's classic horror films, James Whale's 1932 *The Old Dark House*.

Basically, Rohauer operated under the principle of the Big Lie. He bent and used every loophole of the law to his own advantage—and when business opponents used the same loopholes, he descended on them with wrathful press releases and a battery of lawyers. This was a useful technique in the television industry. TV stations didn't want lawsuits that could upset programming and delay or derail announced films. It was easier to settle. The more settlements Rohauer won, the more precedents he could cite in his favor. Even when he *lost* a lawsuit, as he did once with the Paul Killiam group, owners of the D. W. Griffith estate, he would claim (especially to overseas parties) that he had won. On one memorable occasion involving the showing of Griffith's *Intolerance* at

Dan Talbot's New Yorker Theater, he signed a firm contract one day, verbally reneged the next, pulled in his horns when called to account, and then reneged *again* verbally the very next day.

Virtually everybody involved in the use of silent or archival film had their individual showdowns with Rohauer. One of the oft-relished highlights of his career was a long editorial that the *London Times* devoted to denouncing him and his methods; far from repudiating the contents, Rohauer's delighted response was to shower the *Times* and the author of the piece with a libel suit for several million dollars; he also sued, for similar amounts, all the people he *assumed* had provided information for the article. My own initial run-in with the gentleman was when he tried to ingratiate himself with MGM's legal department, which was suing him over a major infraction, by siccing it onto me for an unlawful film society showing of the original silent *Ben Hur*. FBI agents dutifully sat in on the small screening and confiscated the print, but recognized that it was at best an academic, nonprofit event. The case was almost immediately dropped—although for some time afterward Rohauer delighted in telling anybody who would listen that as a result of his intervention I was languishing in prison awaiting deportation to my native England.

Rohauer's business rivals found coexistence virtually impossible: very few, like Paul Killiam, had the guts to risk a considerable amount of money fighting him in the courts; most usually gave it up as a bad job. Rohauer's staff overhead was small—representatives here and there to handle sales and oversee print storage and shipment. His most valuable assets were his fine-print-trained lawyers, who had a habit of changing periodically when they found his affairs consuming too much of their time. Most of his enemies were not his business competitors but the lovers of old film who, especially in pre-video days, had relatively few archives, institutions, and theaters to provide them with the films they hungered for.

One of Rohauer's more exasperating habits was to buy up whole blocks of film—or by the purchase of a few films, to claim ownership of far more—and then to do nothing with them. He laid claim to the films of Harry Langdon, the silent comedies of slapstick comedian Larry Semon, the entire output of Douglas Fairbanks (though he showed only the most famous films), and similar material. Much of this was of questionable commercial value and it's not surprising that Rohauer did little with it. But when an archive turned up with one of those films, which might well be legally in the public domain, he would pounce, demanding that the screening be canceled and the print surrendered to him. The archives often had a contract with an original donor that precluded them from surrendering the print to a later owner, but in order to ensure their ownership of the print in question, they would usually cancel all future exhibitions of it. Further incensing film audiences, Rohauer frequently made deliberately second-rate prints: first to discourage duping (something he was understandably paranoid about since it was the source of much of his own collection) and second to make sure that any dupes that *were* made would be of such poor quality as to be commercially unusable. This meant that some of the richest gems in the Rohauer collection—films like Fairbanks's silent *Robin Hood*, with its superb sets, art direction, and magnificently nuanced photography— were presented in murky prints where detail was lost in background blackness and facial expressions registered only as white blobs.

A further attempt to "protect" his rights involved *changing* the original films. By rewording and replacing some of the subtitles in Keaton's comedy classics, Rohauer was able legally to create "new" entities that could be recopyrighted—and instantly recognized if illegally duped. Keaton's titling was always minimal, subtle, and respected the intelligence of the audience—a well thought-out punctuation of the film. Change it, and the rhythm of the film was destroyed. With Carl Dreyer's early sound horror classic *Vampyr*, Rohauer decided to improve on Dreyer's suggestively evocative terror—which avoided any of the traditionally visual horror tricks—by inserting all the blood and guts Dreyer had found unnecessary into the subtitles. Since the film was short, he placed his long titles *after* the already long and largely untranslated Danish titles. The result: one *read* his version of *Vampyr* almost as much as one *saw* it. Small wonder that around this time, Rohauer began to be affectionately known as Raw-Horror, and audiences—around the world—hissed in unison when the logo RAYMOND ROHAUER PRESENTS appeared on the screen, followed by his name on the copyright notices, usually printed in larger letters than the star or director of the film. David Shephard, a West Coast archivist and technician, delighted aficionados when he issued, as a parody, Edison's 1893 vignette *The Sneeze*, broken up into segments, each separately copyrighted as if by Rohauer, and carrying a stern warning against anyone sneezing without Rohauer's permission since he carried a copyright on that process too!

One of the more amusing and least harmful of Rohauer's ego-dominated activities was to tote a camera around with him at all times. Whenever he had lunch with, or met, a celebrity, out came that camera, and the victim was posed, often quite unwillingly, with him. In a day or so, the picture would appear in print, protected by a copyright in Rohauer's name.

It would be all too easy—and admittedly very entertaining—to go on and on listing Rohauer's practices, lawsuits, and apparent pursuit of total power. Let's wind up the negative side—and yes, there *is* a positive side too—by citing one last supremely frustrating example. To Rohauer, acquiring rights to a film on paper meant that he had the film in actuality. When, a few years before he died, he acquired nontheatrical release rights to whatever Griffith, Norma Talmadge, and Constance Talmadge material still existed, he immediately issued an ornate, expensively produced catalogue on glossy art paper, listing *all* of their films as being available for rental. Running times were given, rental prices were allocated. No mention was made of the fact that fully half the films no longer existed, and that archives the world over had been searching for years for films like D. W. Griffith's *The Greatest Thing in Life*. His offices accepted bookings, confirmed them, and even had the gall to send invoices for films that had not been sent because they just did not exist. Clearly, all Rohauer wanted out of the deal was that catalogue proving his ownership.

And yet there *was* a positive side to this incredible man. While he wasn't a scholar, he was a shrewd judge of offbeat and unrecognized talent. He espoused the cause of director Albert Lewin, and was responsible for keeping his remarkable *Pandora and the Flying Dutchman* in circulation. Harry Langdon's popularity was brief, probably achieved only because his peak coincided with Chaplin's off-screen years, and he has never been reestablished. He *is* a quirky comedian, an acquired taste, the Carl Dreyer of the clowns, and Rohauer had the acumen to acquire legally all of his First National features and his shorts; their preservation as a body of work is largely due to Rohauer's efforts. Although he had run afoul of Chaplin's people at one time in his career (for showing a retrospective of all of Chaplin's major films without clearance), Rohauer was still able to buy out an entire warehouse of Chaplin outtakes and other unused material, footage that proved to be a minor treasure trove to film historian Kevin Brownlow when he made his genuinely classic TV trilogy *The Unknown Chaplin.* Many of the groups of films Rohauer purchased from lesser producers together with scores of individual films— from Conrad Veidt's German silent *The Hands of Orlac* to the odd, Gothic directorial debut of Terence Young, *Corridor of Mirrors*— have considerable academic and, who knows, perhaps even commercial value, once his Aladdin's cave of treasures is assessed and sold.

One of the ironies, perhaps tragedies, of Rohauer's career is that had the tremendous energy he threw into lawsuits and intrigues been harnessed to the exploitation and exhibition of his collection, he might well have become one of the heroes of the archival preservation movement, instead of one of its chief irritants and villains. In his final year or two, Rohauer mellowed considerably, and, while maintaining access, he donated a lot of valuable 35mm nitrate material to the Library of Congress to ensure its preservation.

The disposition of Rohauer's vast and valuable collection of films has not been finalized. Fortuitously, it rests in the hands of one Richard Gordon, a film producer and a gentleman of the old school who was also smart enough always to be at least one step ahead of Rohauer in his dealings with him, and thus to be one of the few people to earn his trust and respect. The film collection itself is enormous, and since Rohauer was always secretive and didn't necessarily commit all of his holdings to an official listing, it will probably contain all sorts of surprises invaluable in this preservation-conscious era. Whoever finally acquires his material, and digs through all those cans and boxes stored in several large vaults here and in England, may even come across the filmic "Rosebud" to explain what made Rohauer tick.

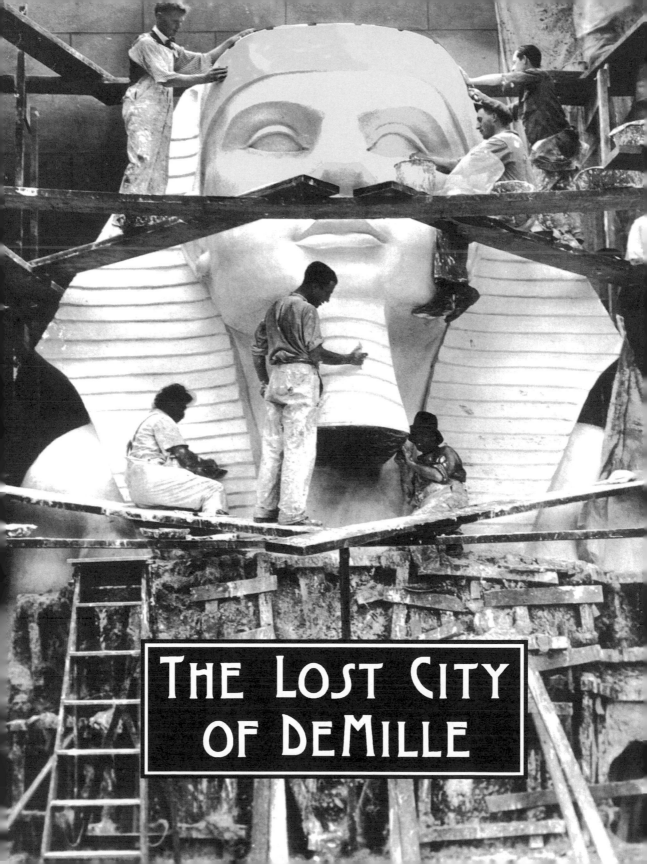

THE LOST CITY OF DEMILLE

IF A THOUSAND YEARS FROM NOW archaeologists happen to dig beneath
the sands of Guadalupe, I hope they do not rush into print with the
amazing news that Egyptian civilization, far from being confined to the
Valley of the Nile, extended all the way to the Pacific coast of North America.

—*Cecil B. DeMille*

Exodus scene from *The Ten Commandments.*

Left to right: Paul Iribe (art director), Cecil B. DeMille (director), and Francis McComas (designer) go over blueprints for the main sets.

Preceding page, opposite and left: Construction of the "Gates of Ramses" and "The Avenue of The Sphinxes."

O N THE ROLLING DUNES OF GUADALUPE, California, in northern Santa Barbara County, Cecil B. DeMille erected one of the largest sets in cinema history for his 1923 silent epic *The Ten Commandments*. Using some 1,600 construction and maintenance workers, 550,000 feet of lumber, 25,000 pounds of nails, 300 tons of plaster, 2,500 actors, and 3,000 animals, the early Technicolor production was budgeted at the then-astronomical figure of $1.4 million. A city of 500 tents ("Camp DeMille") was built to house the cast and crew, just east of the main set—dubbed the City of the Pharaoh. The city itself was over 120 feet high and 800 feet wide and featured 500 tons of replicated Egyptian statuary, including four thirty-five-foot-high statues of Ramses and was fronted by an avenue flanked with twenty-one plaster sphinxes, each weighing five tons. After months of filming, DeMille, over budget, buried the set beneath the dunes—instead of hauling it away as he was contractually required to do—where it remained forgotten for the next sixty-seven years.

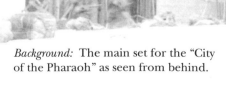

Background: The main set for the "City of the Pharaoh" as seen from behind.

Left to right: Theodore Roberts as Moses greets a rabbi (consultant on Biblical history) and director Cecil B. DeMille.

Top to bottom: Two of the four statues of Ramses which flanked the main entrance to the City of the Pharaoh. Modeled after those at Abu Simbel in Egypt, they were each made of four tons of modeling clay and 35 tons of plaster.

Artisans put the finishing touches on the head of one of the statues of Ramses.

Sphinxes on their way to the Guadalupe location.

I NTRIGUED BY DEMILLE'S RECOLLECTIONS in his 1959 autobiography, documentary filmmaker Peter Brosnan and his associates Bruce Cardoza and Richard Eberhardt made an initial survey of *The Ten Commandments* site in 1983. In 1990, Brosnan and archaeologist John Parker led a team to Guadalupe to begin a preliminary archaeological excavation of the City of the Pharaoh (abridged for lack of funding).

Background: Peter Brosnan surveys the Guadalupe dunes.

Artifacts, including costume buttons, recovered from the Guadalupe site.

MAP 3
TOPOGRAPHY OF THE SITE AREA
PRELIMINARY CONTOUR MAP

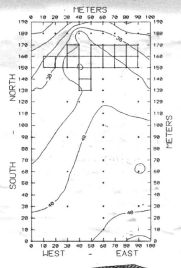

PRELIMINARY SURFACE MAP

VERTICAL DISTANCES EXAGGERATED 4:1

T HROUGH GROUND-PENETRATING RADAR and digitized computer mapping, the survey established that significant portions of the set were intact and recoverable, though threatened by natural erosion (the "DeMille dune" is moving at an average rate of 3.8 feet per year). The expedition then uncovered several of the larger structures (that have now been temporarily reburied) and recovered various smaller artifacts—which were restored and displayed at the Hollywood Studio Museum.

Above: Peter Brosnan and a volunteer examine the face of one of the "charioteer" bas-reliefs from the Ramses Gate portion of the main set.

Left: Computer-generated topographical maps of the Guadalupe site. The smaller grid within the preliminary contour map *(top)* outlines the actual excavated area.

203

Right and opposite lower right: Original props from *The Ten Commandments* in the collection of the Hollywood Studio Museum.

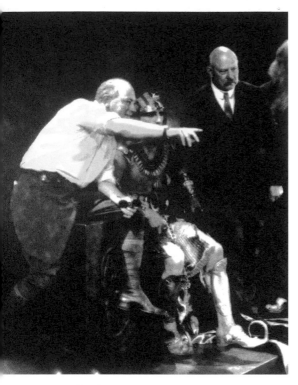

DeMille directs Charles deRoche in the role of Pharaoh.

"CAMP DEMILLE," the tent city erected to house the thousands involved in the making of *The Ten Commandments*, also included a hospital tent, administrative tent, projection-room tent, and a giant mess tent that could seat 1,500. Cast and crew were supplied with food and essentials from nearby towns by a fleet of 132 trucks. A wide avenue separated the men's and women's tents. It was patrolled by a special guard, dubbed "DeMille's Sex Squad" to prevent illicit liaisons and alcohol (and the attendant bad publicity) from tainting this moralistic, Prohibition-era epic.

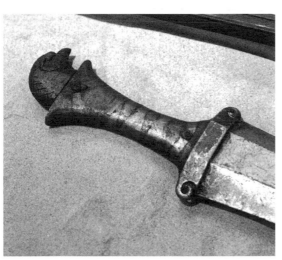

Left: Fragments of a cough-syrup bottle recovered at the site. Cough syrup, with its high codeine content, was a common substitute for alcohol during the Prohibition.

Archaeologist John Parker conducts a survey of the site.

Opposite: Rod LaRocque signs in visitors to the 250th performance of *The Ten Commandments* at Grauman's Egyptian Theatre in Hollywood.

Above: Moses receives the tablets in a scene from *The Ten Commandments.*

Right: A local-history buff and volunteer holds a fragment of colored plaster, one of the thousands that remain from the main set's 120-foot-high walls.

Visitors kindly requested to Sign Their Names in "THE TEN COMMANDMENTS" REGISTRY BOOK

DAMON KRUKOWSKI

The Antediluvian World

Was such a catastrophe possible? The testimony of the sea
is unequivocally yes; catastrophes are continual, commonplace, and require
no great preparation or anterior warning. Geologically speaking,
we are the last of an incalculable number of vast changes,
continents sunk under the ocean while new lands rise on both sides of it.
A loud explosion was heard, and immense columns of boiling mud,
mixed with lapilli, of the size of nuts, were projected from the mountain;
on the following days the rain fell in torrents.

Testimony of the flora and fauna is likewise abundant and irrefutable.
The banana is seedless. Have you never wondered at this? The deluge,
when it comes, is total. The Pacific coast possesses no papaw,
no linden or basswood, no locust trees, no cherry tree large enough for timber,
no gum trees, no sorrel tree, nor kalmia; no persimmon trees,
not a holly, only one ash that may be called a timber tree, no catalpa or
sassafras, not a single elm or hackberry, not a mulberry,
not a hickory, or a beech, or a true chestnut.

Our deluge is not the first; our actual race of man
is not the first. "The earth," says Cosmos, "presses downward,
but the igneous parts tend upward." The sun hangs suspended in between,
hidden behind a crooked mountain at night.

From
Essay on the Jukebox

Even as an adolescent, with his parents, he didn't go to the inn or to have a soda, but to the "Wurlitzer" ("Wurlitzer is Jukebox" was the advertising slogan), to listen to records. . . . Yet the external form of the various devices and even the selections they offered meant at first less than the particular sound emanating from them. This sound did not come from above, as from the radio that stood at home in the corner with the shrine, but from underground, and also, although the volume might be the same, instead of from the usual tinny box, from an inner space whose vibrations filled the room. It was as if it were not an automatic device but rather an additional instrument that imbued the music—though only a certain kind of music, as he realized in retrospect—with its underlying sound, comparable perhaps to the rattling of a train, when it suddenly becomes, as the train passes over an iron bridge, a primeval thunder. Much later, a child was standing one time by such a jukebox (it was playing Madonna's "Like a Prayer," his own selection), the child still so small that the entire force of the loudspeaker down below was directed at his body. The child was listening, all ears, all solemn, all absorbed, while his parents had already reached the door, were ready to leave, calling to the child again and again, and in between smiling at his behavior, as if to apologize for their offspring to the other patrons, until the song had died away and the child, still solemn and reverent, walked past his father and mother onto the street. (Did this suggest that the obelisk-shaped jukeboxes' lack of success had less to do with their unusual appearance than with the fact that the music was directed upward, toward the ceiling?)

. . . He was not satisfied to have the jukeboxes simply stand there; they had to be ready to play, quietly humming—even better than having just been set in motion by a stranger's hand—lit up as brightly as possible, as if from their inner depths; there was nothing more mournful than a dark, cold, obsolete metal box, possibly even shamefacedly hidden from view under a crocheted Alpine throw. Yet that did not quite correspond to the facts, for he now recalled a defective jukebox in the Japanese temple site of Nikko, the first one encountered in that country after a long journey between south and north, hidden under bundles of magazines, the coin slot, covered over with a strip of tape, promptly uncovered by him—but at any rate there, at last. To celebrate this find he had drunk another sake and let the train to Tokyo out there in the darkness depart without him. Before that, at an abandoned temple site way up in the woods, he had passed a still smoldering peat fire, next to it a birch broom and a mound of snow, and farther along in the mountainous terrain a boulder had poked out of a brook, and as the water shot over it, it had sounded just like the water in a certain other rocky mountain brook—as if one were receiving, if one's ears were open to it, the broadcast of a half-sung, half-drummed speech before the plenary session of the United Nations of a planet far off in the universe. Then, at night in Tokyo, people had stepped over others lying every which way on the railroad steps, and even later, again in a temple precinct, a drunk had stopped before the incense burner, had prayed, and then staggered off into the darkness.

It was not only the belly resonance: the "American hits" had also sounded entirely different to him back then on the jukeboxes of his native land than on the radio in his house. He always wanted the radio volume turned up when Paul Anka sang his "Diana," Dion his "Sweet Little Sheila," and Ricky Nelson his "Gypsy Woman," but at the same time he felt guilty that such nonmusic appealed to him (later, when he was at the university and finally had a record player in his room, with the radio as an amplifier, for the first few years it was reserved for what was conventionally felt to deserve the name of music). But from the jukebox he boldly unleashed the trills, howls, shouts, rattling, and booming that not merely gave him pleasure but filled him with shudders of rapture, warmth, and fellowship. In the reverberating steel-guitar ride of "Apache," the cold, stale, and belch-filled Espresso Bar on the highway from the "City of the Plebiscite of 1920" to the "City of the Popular Uprising of 1938" got plugged into an entirely different kind of electricity, with which he could choose, on the glowing scale at hip-level, numbers from "Memphis, Tennessee," feel himself turning into the mysterious "handsome stranger," and hear the rumbling and squeaking of the trucks outside transformed into the steady roar of a convoy on "Route 66," with the thought: No matter where to—just out of here!

Although back home the music boxes had also been a gathering point for Saturday-night dances—a large semicircle around them was usually left clear—he himself would never have thought of joining in. He did enjoy watching the dancers, who in the dimness of the cafés became mere outlines around the massive illuminated case whose rumble seemed to come out of the ground—but for him a jukebox . . . was a source of peace, or something that made one feel peaceful, made one sit still, in relative motionlessness or breathlessness, interrupted only by the measured, positively ceremonial act of "going to push the buttons." And in listening to a jukebox he was never beside himself, or feverish, or dreamy, as he otherwise was with music that affected him—even strictly classical music, and the seemingly rapturous music of earlier eras. The dangerous part about listening to music, someone had once told him, was the propensity it had to make one perceive something that remained to be done as already done. The jukebox sound of his early years, on the other hand, literally caused him to collect himself and awakened, or activated, his images of what might be possible and encouraged him to contemplate them.

The places where one could mull things over as nowhere else sometimes became, during his years at the university, places of evasion, comparable to movie theaters; yet while he tended to sneak into the latter, he would enter his various jukebox cafés in a more carefree manner, telling himself that these proven places of self-reflection were also the right places for studying. This turned out to be a delusion, for once he was alone again, for instance before bedtime, and tried to review the material he had gone over in such a public setting, as a rule he had not retained much. What he owed to those niches or hideouts during the cold years of his university studies were experiences that he now, in the process of writing about them, could only characterize as "wonderful." One evening in late winter he was sitting in one of his trusty jukebox cafés, underlining a text all the more heavily the less he was taking it in. This café was in a rather atypical location for such places, at the edge of the city park, and its glass display cases with pastries and its marble-topped tables were also incongruous. The box was playing, but he was waiting as usual for the songs he had selected; only then was it right. Suddenly, after the pause between records, which, along with those noises—clicking, a whirring sound of searching back and forth through the belly of the device, snapping, swinging into place, a crackle before the first measure—constituted the essence of the jukebox, as it were, a kind of music came swelling out of the depths that made him experience, for the first time in his life, as later only in moments of love, what is technically referred to as "levitation," and which he himself, more than a quarter of a century later, would call . . . what? "epiphany"? "ecstasy"? "fusing with the world"? Or explain thus: "That—this song, this sound—is now me; with these voices, these harmonies, I have become, as never before in life, who I am: as this song is, so am I, complete!" (As usual there was an expression for it, but as usual it was not quite the same thing: "He became one with the music.")

Without at first wanting to know the identity of the group whose voices, carried by the guitars, streamed forth singly, in counterpoint, and finally in unison—previously he had preferred soloists on jukeboxes—he was simply filled with amazement. In the following weeks, too, when he went to the place every day for hours, to sit surrounded by this big yet so frivolous sound that he let the other patrons offer him, he remained in a state of amazement devoid of name-curiosity. (Imperceptibly the music box had become the hub of the Park Café, where previously the most prominent sound had been the rattle of newspaper holders, and the only records that were played, over and over, were the two by that no-name group.) But then, when he discovered one day, during his now-infrequent listening to the radio, what that choir of sassy angelic tongues was called, who, with their devil-may-care

bellowing of "I Want to Hold Your Hand," "Love Me Do," "Roll
Over, Beethoven," lifted all the weight in the world from his shoulders, these became the first "non–serious" records he bought (subsequently he bought hardly any other kind), and then in the café
with columns he was the one who kept pushing the same buttons
for "I Saw Her Standing There" (on the jukebox, of course) and
"Things We Said Today" (by now without looking, the numbers
and letters more firmly fixed in his head than the Ten Commandments), until one day the wrong songs, spurious voices, came nat-
tering out: the management had left the old label and slipped in
the "current hit," in German. . . . And to this day, he thought, with
the sound of the early Beatles in his ear, coming from that Wurlitzer surrounded by the trees in the park: when would the world
see such loveliness again?

In the years that followed, jukeboxes lost some of their mag-
netic attraction for him—perhaps less because he now was more
likely to listen to music at home, and surely not because he was
getting older, but—as he thought he recognized when he got
down to work on the "essay"—because he had meanwhile been
living abroad. Of course he always popped in a coin whenever
he encountered—in Düsseldorf, Amsterdam, Cockfosters, Santa
Teresa Gallura—one of these old friends, eager to be of service,
humming and sparkling with color, but it was more out of habit
or tradition, and he tended to listen with only half an ear. But its
significance promptly returned during his brief stopovers in what
should have been his ancestral region. Whereas some people on
a trip home go first to the cemetery, down to the lake, or to their
favorite café, he not infrequently made his way straight from the
bus station to a music box, in hopes that, properly permeated with
its roar, he could set out on his other visits seeming less foreign
and maladroit.

Yet there were also stories to tell of jukeboxes abroad that had
played not only their records but also a role at the heart of larger
events. Each of these events had occurred not just abroad but at
a border: at the end of a familiar sort of world. If America was, so
to speak, the "home of the jukebox," when he was there none had
made much of an impression on him—except, and there time and
again, in Alaska. But: did he consider Alaska part of the "United
States"? — One Christmas Eve he had arrived in Anchorage, and,

after Midnight Mass, where outside the door of the little wooden church, amid all the strangers, him included, a rare cheerfulness had taken hold, he had gone to a bar. There, in the dimness and confusion of the drunken patrons, he saw, by the glowing jukebox, the only calm figure, an Indian woman. She had turned toward him, a large, proud, yet mocking face, and this would be the only time he ever danced with someone to the pounding of a jukebox. Even those patrons who were looking for a fight made way for them, as if this woman, young, or rather ageless, as she was, were the elder in that setting. Later the two of them had gone out together through a back door, where, in an icy lot, her Land Cruiser was parked, the side windows painted with Alaska pines silhouetted on the shores of an empty lake. It was snowing. From a distance, without their having touched each other except in the lighthandedness of dancing, she invited him to come with her; she and her parents had a fishing business in a village beyond Cook Inlet. And in this moment it became clear to him that for once in his life there was a decision imagined not by him alone but by someone else; and at once he could imagine moving with the strange woman beyond the border out there in the snow, in complete seriousness, for good, without return, and giving up his name, his type of work, every one of his habits; those eyes there, that place, often dreamed of, far from all that was familiar—it was the moment when Percival hovered on the verge of the question that would prove his salvation, and he? on the verge of the corresponding Yes. And like Percival, and not because he was uncertain—he had that image, after all—but as if it were innate and quite proper, he hesitated, and in the next moment the image, the woman, had literally vanished into the snowy night. For the next few evenings he kept going back to the place again and again, and waited for her by the jukebox, then even made inquiries and tried to track her down, but although many remembered her, no one could tell him where she lived. Even a decade later, this experience was one of the reasons he made a point of standing in line all morning for an American visa before flying back from Japan, then actually got off the plane in the wintry darkness of Anchorage and spent several days wandering through the blowing snow in this city to whose clear air and broad horizons his heart was attached. In the meantime nouvelle cuisine had even reached Alaska, and the "saloon" had turned into a "bistro," with the appropriate menu, a rise in status that naturally, and this was to be observed not only in Anchorage, left no room for a heavy, old-fashioned music machine amid all the bright, light furniture. But an indication that one might be present were the figures—of all races—staggering onto the sidewalk from a tubelike barracks, as if from its most remote corner, or outside, among hunks of ice, a person surrounded by a police patrol and flailing around—as a rule, a white male who then, lying on his stomach on the ground, his shoulders, and his shins bent back against his thighs, tightly tied, his hands cuffed behind his back, was slid like a sled along the ice and snow to the waiting police van. Inside the barracks, one could count on being greeted right up front at the bar, on which rested the heads of dribbling and vomiting sleepers (men and women, mostly Eskimos), by a classic jukebox, dominating the long tube of a room, with the corresponding old faithfuls—one would find all the singles of Creedence Clearwater Revival, and then hear John Fogerty's piercing, gloomy laments cut through the clouds of smoke: somewhere in the course of his minstrel's wandering, he had "lost the connection," and "If I at least had a dollar for every song I've sung!" while from down at the railroad station, open in winter only for freight, the whistle of a locomotive, with the odd name for the far north of "Southern Pacific Railway," sent its single, prolonged organ note through the whole city, and from a wire in front of the bridge to the boat harbor, open only in summer, dangled a strangled crow.

Did this suggest that music boxes were something for idlers, for those who loafed around cities, and, in their more modern form, around the world? — No. He, at any rate, sought out jukeboxes less in times of idleness than when he had work, or plans, and particularly after returning from all sorts of foreign parts to the place he came from. The equivalent of walking out to find silence before the hours spent writing was, afterward, almost as regularly, going to a jukebox. — For distraction? — No. When he was on the track of something, the last thing in the world he wanted was to be distracted from it. Over time his house had in fact become a house without music, without a record player and the like; whenever the news on the radio was followed by music, of whatever kind, he would turn it off; also, when time hung heavy, in hours of emptiness and dulled senses, he had only to imagine sitting in front of the television instead of alone, and he would prefer his present state. Even movie theaters, which in earlier days had been a sort of shelter after work, he now avoided more and more. By now he was too often overcome, especially in them, by a sense of being lost to the world, from which he feared he would never emerge and never find his way back to his own concerns, and that he left in the middle of the film was simply running away from such afternoon nightmares. — So he went to jukeboxes in order to collect himself, as at the beginning? — That wasn't it anymore, either. Perhaps he, who . . . had tried to puzzle out the writings of Teresa of Avila, could explain "going to sit" with these objects after sitting at his desk by a somewhat cocky comparison: the saint had been influenced by a religious controversy of her times, at the beginning of the sixteenth century, between two groups, having to do with the best way to move closer to God. One group—the so-called *recogidos*—believed they were supposed to "collect" themselves by contracting their muscles and such, and the others—*dejados*, "leavers" or "relaxers"—simply opened themselves up passively to whatever God wanted to work in their soul, their alma. And Teresa of Avila seemed to be closer to the leavers than to the collectors, for she said that when someone set out to give himself more to God, he could be overwhelmed by the evil spirit—and so he sat by his jukeboxes, so to speak, not to gather concentration for going back to work, but to relax for it. Without his doing anything but keeping an ear open for the special jukebox chords—"special," too, because here, in a public place, he was not exposed to them but had chosen them, was "playing" them himself, as it were—the continuation took shape in him, as he let himself go: images that had long since become lifeless now began to move, needed only to be written down as, next to (in Spanish *junto*, attached to) the music box, he was listening to Bob Marley's "Redemption Songs." And from Alice's "Una notte speciale," played day after day, among other things, an entirely unplanned woman character entered the story on which he was working, and developed in all directions. And unlike after having too much to drink, the things he noted down after such listening still had substance the next day. So in those periods of reflection (which never proved fertile at home, when he tried, at his desk, to force them; he was acquainted with intentional thinking only in the form of making comparisons and distinctions), he would set out to walk not only as far as possible but also out to the jukebox joints. When he was sitting in the pimps' hangout, whose box had once been shot at, or in the café of the unemployed, with its table for patients out on passes from the nearby mental hospital—silent, expressionless palefaces, in motion only for swallowing pills with beer—no one wanted to believe him that he had come not for the atmosphere but to hear "Hey Joe" and "Me and Bobby McGee" again. — But didn't that mean that he sought out jukeboxes in order to, as people said, sneak away from the present? — Perhaps. Yet as a rule the opposite was true: with his favorite object there, anything else around acquired a presentness all its own. Whenever possible he would find a seat in such joints from which he could see the entire room and a bit of the outside. Here he would often achieve, in consort with the jukebox, along with letting his imagination roam, and without engaging in the observing he found so distasteful, a strengthening of himself, or an immersion in the present, which applied to the other sights as well. And what became present about them was not so much their striking features or their particular attractions as their ordinary aspects, even just the familiar forms or colors, and such enhanced presentness seemed valuable to him—nothing more precious or more worthy of being passed on than this; a sort of heightened awareness such as otherwise occurs only with a book that stimulates reflection. So it meant something, quite simply, when a man left, a branch stirred, the bus was yellow and turned off at the station, the intersection formed a triangle, the chalk was lying at the edge of the pool table, it was raining, and, and, and. Yes, that was it: the present was equipped with flexible joints! . . .

Music boxes also made themselves known in their menu of choices; with a hodgepodge of machine- and handwritten notations, and, above all, handwriting that changed from title to title, one in block letters, in ink, the next in flowing, almost stenographic secretary style, but most, even with the most dissimilar loops and slants of the letters, showing signs of particular care and seriousness, some, like children's handwriting, as if painted, and, time and again, among all the mistakes, correctly written ones (with proper accents and hyphens), song titles that must have struck the waitress in question as very foreign, the paper here and there already yellowed, the writing faded and hard to make out, perhaps also taped over with freshly written labels with different titles, but where it showed through, even if illegible, still powerfully suggestive. In time, his first glance more and more sought out those records in a jukebox's table of choices that were indicated in such handwriting, rather than "his" records, even if there were only one such. And sometimes that was the only one he listened to, even if it had been unfamiliar or completely unknown to him beforehand. Thus, in a North African bar in a Paris suburb, standing in front of a jukebox (whose list of exclusively French selections immediately made it recognizable as a Mafia product), he had discovered on the edge a label, handwritten, in very large, irregular letters, each as emphatic as an exclamation point, and had selected that smuggled-in Arab song, then again and again, and even now he was still haunted by that far-resonating "Sidi Mansur," which the bartender, rousing himself from his silence, told him was the name of "a special, out-of-the-ordinary place" ("You can't just go there!").

— Was that supposed to mean that he regretted the disappearance of his jukeboxes, these objects of yesteryear, unlikely to have a second future? — No. He merely wanted to capture and acknowledge, before even he lost sight of it, what an object could mean to a person, above all what could emanate from a mere object. — An eating place by a playing field on the outskirts of Salzburg. Outdoors. A bright summer evening. The jukebox is outside, next to the open door. On the terrace, different patrons at every table, Dutch, English, Spanish, speaking their own languages, for the place also serves the adjacent campgrounds, by the airfield. It is the early eighties, the airfield has not yet become "Salzburg Airport," the last plane lands at sundown. The trees between the terrace and the playing field are birches and poplars, in the warm air constant fluttering of leaves against the deep yellow sky. At one table the locals are sitting, members of the Maxglan Working Man's Athletic Club with their wives. The soccer team, at that time still a second-division club, has just lost another game that afternoon, and will probably be dropped from the league. But now, in the evening, those affected are talking about the trees for a change, while there is a constant coming and going at the window where beer is dispensed—from the tents and back. They look at the trees:

how big they've gotten and how straight they've grown, since they, the club members, went out and with their own hands dug them up as seedlings from the black mossy soil and planted them here in rows in the brown clay! The song that the jukebox sends out again and again that evening into the gradually oncoming darkness, in the pauses between the rustling and rasping of the leaves and the even buzz of voices, is sung in an enterprising voice by Helene Schneider, and is called "Hot Summer Nites." The place is completely empty inside, and the white curtains billow in at the open windows. Then at some point someone is sitting inside, in a corner, a young woman, silently weeping.

— Years later. A restaurant, a *gostilna*, on the crown of the Yugoslavian karst, at some remove from the highway from Stanjel (or San Danicle del Carso). Indoors. A mighty old-fashioned jukebox next to a cupboard, on the way to the restroom. Visible behind ornamental glass, the record carousel and turntable. To operate it, one uses tokens instead of coins, and then it is not enough to push a button, of which there is only one; first one has to turn a dial until the desired selection lines up with the indicator arrow. The mechanical arm then places the record on the turntable with an elegance comparable to the elbow flourish with which an impeccably trained waiter presents a dish. The *gostilna* is large, with several dining rooms, which on this evening in early fall—while outside the *burja* or *bora* blasts without relief over the highland, coming from the mountains in the north—are full, mostly with young people: an end-of-term party for several classes from all the republics of Yugoslavia; they have met one another for the first time here, over several days. Once the wind carries the distinctive signal of the karst train down from the cliffs, with the dark sound of a mountain ferry. On the wall, across from the customary picture of Tito, hangs an equally colorful but much larger portrait of an unknown: it is the former proprietor, who took his own life. His wife says he was not from around here (even if only from the village in the next valley). The song, selected this evening by one student after another, that wafts through the dining rooms over and over again is sung in a self-conscious and at the same time childishly merry unison, even, as an expression of a people, danceable, and has one word as its refrain: "Jugoslavija!"

— Again years later. Again a summer evening, before dusk,

this time on the Italian side of the karst, or, to be precise, the border of the limestone base, once heaved out to the sea of the cliffless lowlands, here marked by the tracks of the railroad station of Monfalcone. Just beyond it, the desert of stones that rises toward the plateau, concealed along this section of track by a small pine forest—on this side the station, surrounded by the abruptly different vegetation of cedars, palms, plane trees, rhododendron, along with the requisite water, pouring plentifully from the station fountain, whose spigot no one has bothered to turn off. The jukebox stands in the bar, under the window which is wide open after the heat of the day; likewise open, the door leading out to the tracks. Otherwise, the place is almost entirely without furniture; what little there is has been shoved to one side, and they are mopping up already. The lights of the jukebox are reflected in the wet terrazzo floor, a glow that gradually disappears as the floor dries. The face of the barmaid appears very pale at the window, in contrast to those of the few passengers waiting outside, which are tanned. After the departure of the Trieste-Venice Express, the building appears empty, except that on a bench two adolescent boys are tussling, yelling at the top of their voices; the railroad station is their playground at the moment. From the darkness of the pines of the karst, swarms of moths are already issuing forth. A long, sealed freight train rattle-pounds by, the only bright spot against the outside of the cars being the little lead seals blowing behind on their cords. In the stillness that follows—it is the time between the last swallows and the first bats—the sound of the jukebox is heard. The boys tussle a bit longer. Not to listen, but probably quite by chance, two railroad officials come out of their offices to the platform, and from the waiting room comes a cleaning woman. Suddenly figures, previously overlooked, appear all over the scene. On the bench by the beech a man is sleeping. On the grass behind the restrooms, soldiers are stretched out, a whole group, without a trace of luggage. On the platform to Udine, leaning against a pillar, a huge black man, likewise without luggage, in only shirt and pants, engrossed in a book. From the thicket of pines behind the station swoops again and again, one following close upon the other, a pair of doves. It is as if all of them were not travelers but inhabitants or settlers in the area around the railroad station. Its midpoint is the fountain, with its foaming drinking water, blown and spattered by the breeze, and tracks on the asphalt from many wet soles, to which the last drinker now intentionally adds his own. A bit farther down the tracks, accessible on foot, the subterranean karst river, the Timavo, comes to the surface, with three branches, which, in Virgil's time, according to the *Aeneid*, were still ninc; it immediately broadens out and empties into the Mediterranean. The song the jukebox is playing tells of a letter written by a young woman who has ended up far away from her home and from everything she ever knew or dreamed of, and is now full of brave and perhaps also sorrowful astonishment; it floats out into the dusky railroad land of Monfalcone in the friendly voice of Michelle Shocked, and is called "Anchorage, Alaska."

Translated from the German by Krishna Winston

Marea del silencio–41

It is the hour of roots and yellow dogs.
A man wears his silence like a mask;
ivy grows over his eyes.

It is the hour of roots and yellow dogs;
the hour when the whitest horses
run like a chill deep in the mist.

I hear like an absence the mystery close by;
I hear night turn its head
like music.

It is the hour of roots and yellow dogs;
in her crystal palace
the moon clasps her head and weeps.
A man wears his silence like a mask;
he dreams deep under water.

It is the hour when naked bodies shiver,
the hour when the mystery to come or not to come weeps;
the moon is the pain of that absence
before the cruel and clenched, white teeth of men.

It is the hour of roots and yellow dogs,
of clear roots at the bottom of seas,
of mad dogs fleeing
through large, white rooms.

It is the hour of the mystery that comes and does not come,
the hour when night flees from the naked sea,

the hour when birds flee from every statue,
the hour of silver eyelids,
the hour when the moon hums like a silence:
nothing.

Translated from the Spanish by Martin Paul and José A. Elgorriaga

Monster

Photographs by Daniel Faust

Text by Mike Kelley

Captions by Forrest J Ackerman

Forrest J Ackerman, former editor of *Famous Monsters of Filmland* magazine, has the largest existing collection of horror and fantasy film special-effects objects, displayed in his home in the Hollywood Hills. Touring it is like walking through a morgue. Everywhere there are recognizable fragments of Hollywood film reality. Unlike a normal museum where things are organized in a seemingly logical way, his collection is organized like a child's bedroom—things are heaped everywhere in a junkpile of film history.

Mutant from *Beneath The Planet of the Apes* takes a nap in Ackerman's anteroom.

(Foreground) Cat Woman from *Batman Returns*,
Frankenstein bath-soap container, model of dwarf
actor who played a Martian and model of Martian
from *Invasion of the Saucer Men*, model of the She
Creature, model of Frankenstein monster.
(Background) Model of Ackerman's comic-book
creation, Vampirella.

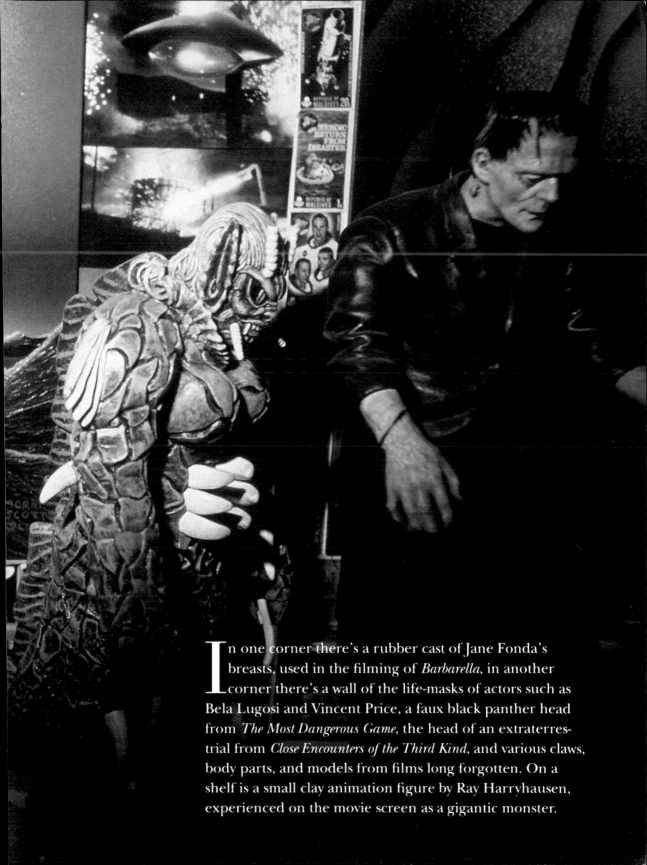

In one corner there's a rubber cast of Jane Fonda's breasts, used in the filming of *Barbarella*, in another corner there's a wall of the life-masks of actors such as Bela Lugosi and Vincent Price, a faux black panther head from *The Most Dangerous Game*, the head of an extraterrestrial from *Close Encounters of the Third Kind*, and various claws, body parts, and models from films long forgotten. On a shelf is a small clay animation figure by Ray Harryhausen, experienced on the movie screen as a gigantic monster.

Jumble of horror heads in alcove. Japanese plaque *(background)* is equivalent of the American "Hugo" award (science fiction's Oscar).

228

Against the backdrop of a painting by Morris Scott Dollens of the Starship Enterprise (from *Star Trek*), a model robot from Disney's *The Black Hole*, the Metaluna Mutant from *This Island Earth* and a model of Gort from the classic scientifilm *The Day The Earth Stood Still*.

The Gas Bomb that brought down King Kong in 1933 stands at the base of the stop-motion brontosaurus model (built by Marcel Delgado, animated by Willis O'Brien) that tipped over the raft with Carl Denham and his camera crew in the lagoon on Skull Island.

Fantasticonglomeration in one of the Ackermuseum's 18 rooms (before 1994 earthquake).

Series of French science-fiction novels.

(Center) The Golem, from oft-filmed story of the Czech Man of Clay who is brought to life by necromancy. *(Right)* Scene from the 1930s version of Poe's *The Black Cat*, co-starring Karloff and Lugosi, front page of newspaper announcing death of Lon Chaney, Sr., *Tales From the Ackermansion* (forthcoming film), *Dante's Inferno* poster (one of the earliest films—1924—Ackerman recalls seeing), *Just Imagine* advertisement.

(Top row) Metal face of 1930s giant ape, White Pongo, *Planet of the Apes* face piece, Ray Harryhausen's animation model of elephant in *20 Million Miles to Earth*, Conrad Veidt mask of *The Man Who Laughs*. *(Middle row)* James Arness head as The Thing and Max Schreck as Nosferatu (the silent Dracula). *(Front row)* Alien head from *Close Encounters*, bronze of Lon Chaney Sr. as the Phantom of the Opera, TV alien, bust of Ultima Futura Automaton, the *Metropolis* robotrix.

Wimpy, Popeye's hamburger-munching friend, rides a Golden Dragon.

Upstairs in the living room is a one-eyed blob *(right)* from an episode of the science-fiction television series *Outer Limits*. This prop is close to five feet high, yet I remember it as having microscopic proportions on the TV show. You realize that, in the movie theater, to experience the projected figures on the screen as life-size is to reduce yourself to the size of a doll; and on television you must mentally blow yourself up to the size of a giant to account for the minuscule scale of the figures on the screen. All of this hits home when you are confronted with Ackerman's collection of objects never meant to be seen in the light of day, but only in the palaces of daydreams. These "statues" refuse to give up their dream to reality. They do not let you return to consciousness too easily. They are too familiar as intensely felt memory to simply become objects.

(Top) Rick Baker's re-creation of Linda Blair in *The Exorcist*, Charles Laughton as Quasimodo, half a dozen interpretations of Frankenstein, including (with glasses) the FrankenForry Monster (FJA in the morning before he has his first cup of coffee). *(Background)* Rare, early limited edition of Edgar Allan Poe's *The Raven*.

(Left) The Thing in the Shoebox from the "Don't Open till Doomsday" episode of TV's *Outer Limits*.

(p. 232)
(Top row) Boris Karloff (1931 at the time he gained his fame as the Frankenstein monster), Ackerman claims, "This is me when I was alive," Bela "Dracula" Lugosi.
(Middle row) Vincent Price, Tor Johnson, John Carradine, Lon Chaney, Jr.
(Bottom row) Life masks of Peter Lorre, Glenn Strange, Don Post, Charles Laughton.

(p. 233)
If Ackerman is to be believed, this is what the major quake did to one of his clocks. It is actually based on a Salvador Dali design.

Scoring Hitchcock

Bernard Herrmann was born in New York in 1911 and studied at New York University and Juilliard. An early champion of the music of Charles Ives, he started working for the Columbia Broadcasting System in 1933 and soon began collaborating with Orson Welles on his radio programs, including the now-famous "War of the Worlds" broadcast in October 1938. In the fall of '39, Welles, invited to Hollywood by RKO Studios, asked Herrmann to come with him to score his first film, *Citizen Kane.*

In 1955, Hitchcock hired Herrmann to compose the music for *The Trouble With Harry.* Herrmann then scored *The Man Who Knew Too Much* (in which he appeared as the orchestra conductor during the climactic assassination attempt at London's Albert Hall). *Vertigo* followed, and *North by Northwest*—for which Herrmann created what he called a "rapid, kaleidoscopic, virtuoso orchestral fandango."

Herrmann insisted on personally orchestrating every note of his film scores (a significant departure from common studio practice—composers would generally "sketch" several lines of a score and leave the detailed orchestration to other staff writers). "[Hitchcock] only finishes a picture 60 percent," he told one interviewer, "I have to finish it for him."

Their most famous collaboration came in 1960 with *Psycho.* Hitchcock shot *Psycho* in five weeks, without name actors, on a budget of $800,000. The music budget was minimal and Herrmann composed a score that required only a string section. "In using only strings," he explained, "I was able to complement the black-and-white photography of the film with a black-and-white sound." "Thirty–three percent of the effect of *Psycho*," Hitchcock later admitted, "was due to the music."

Hitchcock had actually given specific instructions to leave the now-famous shower scene, in which Janet Leigh is knifed to death by Anthony Perkins, unscored. Watching it during dubbing, however, he was disappointed by its lack of impact and Herrmann convinced him to reconsider. In the final version, the only sounds heard are those of running water, Janet Leigh's screams and what musicologist Fred Steiner termed "the shrill, stabbing thrusts of the strings, playing in their topmost registers." (There are no "bird cries," as some critics have suggested.)

The two fell out over the scoring of *Torn Curtain* in 1966 when Herrmann defied Hitchcock's request for a score with "a beat and a rhythm" to appeal to younger audiences. Herrmann died in December 1975, hours after completing the recording of his score for Martin Scorsese's *Taxi Driver.*

—Jon Burlingame

The Murder

Bob,

A friendly note, which I hope
you'll take in the spirit in
which it is written:

Without trying to pull any sort
of rank on you, I must point out
that, being old enough to be your
grandfather, it is, generally
speaking, more comfortable all
around is I am not addressed by
my first name except by close
friends, or at my invitation...

OW

ARTS' DELICATESSEN IS ON VENTURA BLVD...
A BLOCK AND A HALF WEST OF LAUREL CANYON...

PLEASE BRING FROM THERE:

12 SLICES OF ROAST BEEF
12 SLICES OF TONGUE
6 SLICES OF TURKEY

_____

ALSO PLEASE BRING A COPY OF THE L.
AND THE L.A. EXAMINER

_____

_____

I MUST BE AT MA MAISON
AT TWELVE TWENTY...

SO BE SURE YOU ARE BACK HE
TEN TO TWELVE ...

GROCERIES (GOURMET CHALET ON SUNSET
OPEN-- OTHERWISE SUPER-MARKETS, ETC.

X 6 LARGE CANS OF CAMPBELLS CHUNY BEEF   K
X 6 LARGE CANS OF CAMPBELLS CHUNKY CHICK
X 1 ROASTED CHICKEN
X 2 PACKAGES OF HEBREW NATIONAL (OR OTHER
    LEAN BEEF) BRATWURST
  1 LARGE PACKAGE OF BEST GRUYERE OR SWIS
                                      CHE
  4 ENDIVES (IF AVAILABLE)
  4 BUNCHES OF SPRING ONIONS (IF AVAILABLE
X 2 QUARTS OF BEST QUALITY VANILLA ICE CREA
  1 PACKAGE OF RYE CRISP
X 1 PEPPRIDGE FARM (OR SARAH LEE) CARROT CA
  9 SLICES OF ROAST BEEF
  9 SLICES OF TONGUE
  6 SLICES OF HAM
  1 DOZEN BEST QUALITY EGGS
X 2 CANS OF ROAST BEEF HASH
X 4 CANS OF STUFFED CABBAGE
    (this will be available if the GOURMET
     CHALET on Sunset is open today)
  1 T BONE STEAK
  2 BOXES OF LOW FAT COTTAGE CHEESE
X 4 SMALL CONTAINERS OF PLAIN LOW FAT YOGURT
  6 LEMONS
  1 PECAN PIE (HOUSE OF PIES?... IF NOT
    AVAILABLE, GET BANANA CREAM)
X 1 BOX OF TRISKITS
  1 LARGE JAR OF CHUNKY PEANUT BUTTER
  4 CANS OF PRE-MIXED MARGARITA COCKTAILS

_____

MAGAZINES:

NEW WEST
NEW TIMES
NEWSWEEK
TIME
LOS ANGELES SUNDAY TIMES
TV GUIDE

ROBERT KENSINGER with KRISTINE McKENNA

Orson on Wonderland

In 1978, when I was twenty-two, I moved to L.A. to break into the movie business. I arrived here with zero money and no place to live, and for a while I drove a meat truck. Then one day early in 1980 a neighbor of mine told me she knew someone who'd been working for Orson Welles, so I tracked the guy down. He didn't say a word about how hard it was to work for Orson, he just asked me if I was interested and I said definitely.

Citizen Kane had been out of circulation for most of the '50s and '60s, but it came back big when I was a film student at the Rhode Island School of Design in the mid-'70s. There were posters for it plastered all over the campuses at Brown and RISD, and I remember thinking that it looked like a really cheesy production. I went to see it anyway and was blown away. We were used to seeing European movies in film school, which were great, and Hollywood movies, which were almost uniformly lousy, but *Citizen Kane* was something entirely different. The camera work was amazing, and everything about it was so inventive and fresh. I made a point of seeing all of Welles's other films and by the time I graduated I had it in my head that I wanted to work for him.

After a few phone calls, I went to KCOP, where Orson was taping a talk/magic show with Burt Reynolds and Angie Dickinson. Orson had rented the studio space and was footing the bill for the shoot, but he wasn't there when I arrived and I ended up talking to Burt Reynolds and Orson's companion and collaborator,

Oja Kodar. They knew why I was there and I got the feeling that I would have the job if they approved me. After about ten minutes of small talk they handed me the keys to Orson's huge Chrysler convertible, which was parked outside in the lot, and told me to go up to his house and get him.

Orson always rode around with the top down, and he'd had the seats electrified so he could get in and out easily. He hadn't driven in about fifteen years because he'd been ticketed so many times for speeding that he'd permanently lost his license. (He claimed he'd driven to the studio in a horse and carriage for a while.) Anyhow, I drove this boat of a car up to his house on Wonderland Avenue in Laurel Canyon. I couldn't believe where he was living. He was renting a crummy little tract house, one of those early '60s sloped hard-edged buildings. It was such a shabby, unemotional piece of architecture. I rang the bell, and as I stood there waiting, I looked around and noticed that there were hundreds of cigars piled up in the garden, which was mostly dead. I later learned that whenever Orson went into the house he'd throw his cigar in the yard, creating these mounds of cigars everywhere. He only smoked Macanudos, which cost a fortune, and he'd smoke them only halfway before tossing them in the yard.

After what seemed like a long time, the door opened a crack, a hand jutted out holding a pair of shoes, and a voice said, "Please put these in the car." I followed these instructions and returned to the door. This time some clothes on hangers were thrust out and the voice said, "I'll be right out." So I waited in the car for a while before the door finally opened and there he was. His face was a complete blank as he walked out to the car, and he didn't say a word after he got in. I said "Hello," he said "Hello," then he said, "Shall we go?" I tried to make small talk as we drove along, but he said, "Can we please not talk?" I thought, "Oh man, this sucks, I'm gonna quit today." But after we got to the studio and he'd done an interview with Burt Reynolds, he came over to me and was the soul of amiability. "Please come back tomorrow," he said, so I did.

In general, he was pretty vague about what I was supposed to be doing for him and I found that frustrating. I definitely didn't want to be his valet, and fortunately those duties fell to another guy who was working for him. Alan was a young guy from the San Fernando Valley who only knew Orson from talk shows and commercials, and was only there to save enough money to buy a car. He never stopped bitching about Orson, who meant absolutely nothing to him. Orson *was* a major pain in the ass, but I was awed by his talent. Alan talked about him with zero reverence, and he did really malicious things to him. If Orson was looking for a shirt from the cleaners and Alan was too lazy to go get it, he'd tell Orson the cleaners had lost the shirt. On one of my first days working with Orson, we were all sitting in the front room and Orson asked Alan to bring him a pair of scissors. It was hard for Orson to get in and out of chairs, and Alan, who was just flipping through a magazine, hollered back, "What for?" Orson looked at me, then at the kid, and answered, "So I can stab you with them."

Orson hired me because he hated this other guy and wanted me to replace him, but I made it clear that I didn't want to be an errand boy. Orson said, "Fine, I'll keep you with me and put him on shit duty." So the other guy did the shopping and took care of his clothes, and I was with Orson all the time. Orson paid me well—I got about $400 a week, which was pretty good at the time—and I was always paid in cash. He never used checks or credit cards because his finances were a mess. The way he spent money was one of the most eccentric things about him. He'd blow it right and left. He wasn't materialistic, but he never hesitated to get anything he wanted at any given moment. He'd spend until his money ran out, then do something to get more. Almost every penny he spent went toward his work. At the time I was working for him, he had just made a ton of money on those Paul Masson wine commercials—I think he got half a million dollars for them and he did them in three weeks.

My usual routine was to show up at his house at nine or ten in the morning. Orson worked every day and was never idle. He was about sixty then, but he had stamina like you wouldn't believe. This was doubly impressive when you consider that he weighed 350 pounds. He seemed to be in good health, but he went to a doctor once a week. He had back problems, which he never complained about despite the fact that he was often on his feet for twelve hours when we were working, and he had high blood pressure. But he just kept on slugging away. He never took any prescription medication that I knew of, or any other kind of drug. He wasn't supposed to drink, but he'd often knock back three double zombies with dinner. I never saw him drunk, though—he held his liquor very well. (He once told me that when he was shooting *Touch of Evil* in Venice he'd had to do a scene where he fell into one of the canals: "If you think it's dirty now," he told me, "you should have seen it then—it was absolutely filthy." He fell in head first and inhaled all this disgusting water, and when he got out he was so miserable that he got a fifth of gin and downed the whole thing. "I felt so polluted," he explained, "that I had to clean out my system.")

I was supposed to have two days off a week, but Orson would call at any hour of the night or day if he wanted to do something. He'd often say, "I have something to do tomorrow—I'll call you in the afternoon." It drove me nuts because I never knew when I'd be free. Still, I never got over how surreal it was being twenty-two years old and living in Hollywood, and having Orson Welles call me every day. He'd get up at seven each morning, put on his bathrobe and go straight to the typewriter. He had a little sitting area at a window in the front of the house surrounded by a wall of books where he kept a Smith-Corona typewriter. It was a horrible, claustrophobic little space, but he had a big comfortable padded chair, and he'd sit there typing. He'd type my agenda for the day and type notes to people who might be interested in putting money into *The Other Side of the Wind*, the film he was trying to complete at the time. It starred John Huston as an aging, washed-up Hollywood director, with Peter Bogdanovich, Jack Nicholson, Oja Kodar, and others costarring. The film was never released because the negative somehow came to be owned by the government of Iran, and despite all of Orson's efforts, he could never get it back. So, he'd sit there doing paperwork for that film and sometimes he actually wrote. He had a couple of scripts going at the time, and he had completed one called *The Deep* that he wanted to direct and sent out a lot, but he was mostly involved in the magic shows and TV specials he was financing on his own. (He completed three or four of them but I don't think he ever sold any of them.) Orson was an adequate magician but his real skill was as a storyteller—he'd take the simplest trick and draw you into it with a wonderful, mysterious story.

Orson's house was small, with a brown carpet, a flagstone fireplace, and a sloped ceiling with beams going across it. There were no mementos and no art on the walls, and it felt almost like a hotel room. He didn't do anything to leave a personal mark on the place. It was very dark and the living room had a reclining Barcalounger where he'd sometimes sit and watch TV. He watched *All in the Family* religiously. He thought it was the best piece of TV programming ever, and he'd just crack up at Meathead. He never played music at home and if I turned on the radio in the car, he immediately turned it off. He never went to a movie or rented a video, and he never entertained. I got the impression he didn't want people to know where he lived—not because he was ashamed, but because he was bitter and cynical about being in Hollywood. He loved Europe and hated L.A., and often said that if it weren't for the money he'd never set foot here again. He grumbled about the smog in L.A. and called the people in Beverly Hills "mummies." When we were driving, he'd look at them and snarl, "Cadavers—there's no sign of life there." But he courted them, of course, when he needed to raise money.

To the back of the house were Orson's bedroom and bathroom. On his dresser he had a line of fake thumbs for hiding things in magic tricks, his change purse, and a bottle of Jean Naté body splash. When I think of Orson, that's what comes to mind—the smell of cigars and Jean Naté. His closet was filled with twenty or thirty very expensive, identical black cotton shirts with large side and breast pockets that reminded me of Captain Kangaroo. He had them custom-made by an Italian tailor with a shop on Sunset Boulevard across from the Chateau Marmont. Orson never spoke about his body—it was a taboo subject. People used to say to me, "He must eat all day," but he didn't. In fact, we'd go through ten-hour runs of work and he wouldn't eat a thing, but when he did eat, he ate for five people.

His bathtub was filled with a heap of old encyclopedias and bibles. He wasn't religious, but he loved ancient literature and history. He knew the classics and was almost an Elizabethan character himself. Often I'd be talking about something and would suddenly realize that he just wasn't relating. He wasn't in the contemporary world at all, and being with him was like entering a time warp. He saw Hollywood as it had been in the '40s and '50s, and he probably did things in 1980 exactly as he'd done them in 1945.

Next to his room was a room for Oja Kodar, who was an artist.

She made these amorphous, organic-looking plaster sculptures, very late '60s, Claes Oldenburgish forms, and there were lots of them around the house. She was a beautiful woman in her early forties and quite exotic-looking. She and Orson did everything together. I think they really loved each other. He was faithful to her. He couldn't really get around on his own, and at that point, I don't think he had the desire to—I think his sex life was essentially over.

I also think he was lonely. Orson wasn't the kind of person who could be alone, and he needed somebody around at all times. Even late at night after we'd been working all day and he'd done a talk show, he'd often drag me to a restaurant rather than go home, and then he'd sit there making small talk for hours. He seemed to keep his friends on a tether, only pulling them in when he needed company. In fact, in all the time I worked for him I never once saw a friend drop by. His phone didn't ring much because everyone had to call him through his lawyer. He had three children but I never saw any of them either, and as far as I know, they never came around. He never went to parties, although he was invited a lot, but when he was trying to raise money he'd dress up and take people to nice restaurants. These people were mostly dentists and lawyers. Every once in a while he'd have meetings at Ma Maison with people like Spielberg, but essentially he was out of the game. The film community wasn't there for him in any way. I think it ostracized him for a few reasons, and first on the list was his reputation for not being able to control money. He never had any accounting whatsoever for what he spent. Other people hated him because he was a prodigy—and, at times, a show-off. It was also widely known in the industry that he was unreliable when it came to completing his films—in the past he'd shot movies, then got acting jobs and taken off before the editing was completed. (From what I heard, the footage he shot in South America—which was recently released as the documentary *It's All True*—was mostly worthless, but Orson made it sound as if he were the victim and the film had been taken away from him.)

Orson treated everybody equally—except if you were working for him, in which case he treated you like a tool. As a boss, he was overbearing, demanding, even selfish. On a set he saw everyone as existing solely to facilitate his creativity. At the same time,

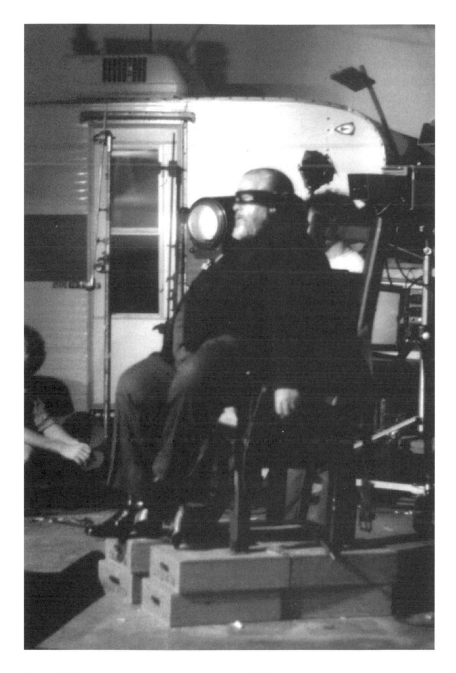

Orson Welles shooting a magic show, circa 1980.

he was very respectful of actors and actresses—he loved Angie Dickinson, for instance, and was also fascinated by Marlene Dietrich. There were plenty of people he had negative opinions of, though. He disliked Joan Collins and thought Greta Garbo was completely vacuous. He also disliked Victor Mature—they were rivals over Rita Hayworth for a while. He despised John Houseman after their Mercury Theater collaboration deteriorated into petty competition for roles on and off the screen. And he never forgave actor Robert Shaw for accidentally burning down his house in Spain and destroying all of his personal mementos.

The most important person in his life was Skipper Hill, who had been the athletics coach and then the headmaster at his school in Woodstock, Illinois, and stayed a mentor/father figure to him for most of his life. Skipper was twenty or thirty years older than Orson, but they were incredibly close. He was a very theatrical man, and, like Orson, he used a vocabulary nobody in the modern world uses. They'd written four textbooks on Shakespeare together. Orson had been fucked over so many times that he didn't trust anybody else. Skipper was his Rock of Gibraltar. His other great love was his dog Blitz, a poodle the size of a baked potato. Orson would spend the day booming in stentorian tones, and the minute he got home and saw Blitz he'd shift into this high-pitched baby talk.

When I first started working for him, I kept asking questions about *Citizen Kane*, but Orson made a rule that I was only allowed to ask one question a week about his past. He rarely answered questions from anybody about *Citizen Kane*. In fact, whenever he did talk shows he'd send a letter in advance instructing them not to bring it up. He wanted to be identified with other films that he was equally proud of. I once asked him who had played Hitler in the opening newsreel footage in *Kane*. He told me that it was a waiter he'd spotted in a restaurant on Hollywood Boulevard. At first the waiter had refused to do the part, so Orson went to dinner there every night and harrassed him into agreeing. When I asked him about the *Kane* sets, which looked to me like some of the most elaborate ever made, he said, "Those are the cheapest sets I ever had. That was a low-budget film and the sets were cardboard." I also asked him about Bernard Herrmann, *Kane*'s music composer, and he fumed, "Hitchcock stole him from me!"

Orson once told me that one of his directing techniques was

to throw a tantrum during the first day on the set. He said he did it as a way of gaining control and letting people know who was boss. I saw him do it many times, at the smallest excuse. Barbara Leaming tells a story about the actor who played Iago in *Othello*; he came up to Orson on the set and just said "Hi" after not having seen him for a while, and Orson absolutely exploded. "Is that how you greet the director of this motion picture? You just say hi?" I witnessed these outbursts many times—with unsuspecting targets. It would quiet a set down in seconds. But the attacks were reserved strictly for men. Even the bimbos he'd use in his magic shows would be treated with kid gloves.

I was the victim of one of his tantrums one night when we were at Lucy's El Adobe having dinner with the crew from a magic show we were shooting. Orson was talking about what an awful actor Dustin Hoffman was and how much he hated method acting, and I countered that *Midnight Cowboy* was one of my favorite films and that Hoffman was great as Ratso Rizzo. Orson always got hostile when he was challenged, and he put down his fork and screamed, "Don't you ever make another cuntish comment like that again!" I stood up and said, "That's my opinion," threw the car keys on the table and walked out. After a while, he came outside and sheepishly handed me the keys and got in the car. I refused to say a word all the way home. When we got to his house he invited me in, and I said, "I'm going home because I'm hungry and tired." He reached in his pocket and handed me fifty dollars and said, "Go have a really great dinner on me." That was the closest he could come to apologizing.

After I'd been working for Orson for about eight months, I quit because I'd been offered a job doing a rewrite on a Roger Corman film. I told him I was going to work on a movie because I had come to L.A. to direct. He said, "Bob, don't waste your time—you'll never be a director. YOU WILL NEVER DIRECT!" I flashed him a look of contempt. I was shocked and he could obviously see it. He added, "It's my duty to tell you how impossible it is to get that job in this town. If you want to direct, go to some small town and make your movie there, but don't waste your time here." I quit anyhow. In parting, he said, "I'll tell you what's going to happen: you'll work for these people, and what-

ever the job you came in with is, that's the job you'll be stuck with. That's the only way they'll ever see you." He was absolutely right, of course. Though I'd been promised various things by the Corman people, they let me go after they'd wrung what they wanted out of me.

A year later I found myself with nothing happening, so I called Orson and asked him if he needed anybody and he hired me again. That was at the beginning of 1980, and I worked for him until the fall, then quit again for good. I just couldn't take the phone calls in the middle of the night anymore. One night shortly before I quit I took Orson over to do the Carson show, and at the end of the evening he was hungry and wanted to get something to eat. When I brought the car around he said, "Somebody stole my money out of the dressing room and now I have no money to eat with." One of the wonderful things about Orson was that as cantankerous as he was, he let any situation roll off his back. I told him I had twelve dollars and he said, "Great, let's go to Pink's," which was a cheap hot dog stand he liked. As we were driving along he suddenly asked me to pull over. "I have an extra pair of pants in the trunk and there's probably some money in the pockets." I found another eight dollars and he said, "Then it's the International House of Pancakes." We were just about to pull into the parking lot when I suddenly remembered that I'd got my first credit card that day. He was ecstatic. "Why didn't you say so!" he said. "That means it's Don the Beachcomber!" which was his favorite restaurant. At Don's, everybody greeted him: he was shown to his favorite table, and they brought him his gold, engraved chopsticks, which were enshrined in a case in the middle of the room with the chopsticks of other famous people.

As we were eating we noticed a family across the room staring at us and eventually the father sent his son over for an autograph. Orson was cordial and he waved to the family across the room. As we were driving home, we saw the same family walking down Hollywood Boulevard. Orson said, "Look at that family. They all love each other, they're all together—what lucky, lucky people," and he didn't say another word for the rest of the ride home. He was incredibly melancholy that night, and I saw a side of him I'd never seen before.

The last time I saw him was in 1981 on my last day at work. I don't know what he did in the four years after I stopped working for him, but I don't think much happened. I know he moved out of the house in Laurel Canyon and bought a house in Beverly Hills that was said to be bigger and nicer. He died in 1985. Though some of my friends at the time made fun of me for being Orson's "slave," when I hear his voice in a sound bite now, or see him on film or TV, I'm not impartial in the way a stranger might be. His dramatic presence, the resonant voice, conjure up real memories of the time I spent with Orson Welles.

Forrest J Ackerman has been a fantasy fan for seventy–two years. "I wasted the first five years of my life," he says, "till I discovered 'imagi-movies' in 1922." He edits *Famous Monsters of Filmland* magazine (begun February 1958) and his literary agency represents two hundred authors of science fiction and fantasy.

Hilton Als is completing a book of essays for Farrar, Straus & Giroux.

John Ashbery's most recent collection of poetry is *And the Stars Were Shining* (Farrar, Straus & Giroux). He teaches at Bard College in New York.

Paul Auster lives in Brooklyn, New York. He is the author of *Leviathan, The New York Trilogy, The Music of Chance* (nominated for the PEN/Faulkner Award), *Moon Palace, In the Country of Last Things, The Invention of Solitude,* and *The Art of Hunger.* "Mr. Vertigo" is an excerpt from his novel of the same name to be published by Viking in August, 1994.

Jon Burlingame is a nationally syndicated media critic. His exhibit "Music in Films: The Sound Behind the Image" recently closed after a year at the Hollywood Bowl Museum in Los Angeles. His first book, on the history of American television scoring, will be published in 1996 by Schirmer Books.

Gabriel Celaya (1911–1991) published some fifty books of poems as well as translations of Rilke and Rimbaud. Aguilar published his *Poesías Completas* in 1969.

Georganne Deen was born in Fort Worth, Texas, in 1951. She has exhibited throughout the United States, most recently as part of "Kustom Kulture: Von Dutch, Big Daddy Roth, Robert Williams and Others" at the Laguna Beach Art Museum and "Comic Power" at Exit Art in New York. Solo exhibitions of her work have been held at Fred Hoffman Gallery and Zero One in Los Angeles. She lives and works in Los Angeles. Her portfolio, *The Take of the Town,* was created for *Grand Street.*

Charles Desmarais was, until recently, director of the Laguna Art Museum, which in 1993 presented "Kustom Kulture," a survey of the influence of the custom-car and underground-comics scene on contemporary Californian art. He resides in Laguna Beach, California.

John Gregory Dunne lives in New York. "Playland—Setting the Scene" is taken from his tenth book, *Playland,* which Random House will publish in August, 1994.

CONTRIBUTORS

William Eggleston was born in Memphis, Tennessee, in 1939. His published collections of photography include *The Democratic Forest, Graceland, William Eggleston's Guide,* and *Morals of Vision.* He lives and works in Memphis. His portfolio of photographs in this issue was commissioned by *Grand Street.*

William K. Everson teaches film history at New York University and the New School of Social Research. He has directed film festivals in Santa Fe, Kentucky, and Telluride, and has participated in the production of documentaries on Charlie Chaplin, Buster Keaton, and D. W. Griffith. He is the author of *American Silent Film, The Films of Laurel & Hardy,* and *The Art of W. C. Fields.*

Daniel Faust has amassed a total of 12,500 slides since 1982 from which he draws his work. A forthcoming book will include 5,000 photos, and a wall-work-in-progress uses 10,000 images. He has exhibited throughout the United States and Europe, including recent solo exhibitions at the Hague Center for Contemporary Art in Holland and American Fine Arts, Co. in New York, which also represents him. He lives and works in New York.

Peter Handke was born in Griffen, Austria, in 1942. He is the author of *The Left-handed Woman, The Goalie's Anxiety at the Penalty Kick, Afternoon of a Writer,* and *Short Letter, Long Farewell.* Handke is also a dramatist, poet, screenwriter, director, and translator. "Essay on the Jukebox" is adapted from his forthcoming book, *The Jukebox and Other Essays on Storytelling,* to be published by Farrar, Straus & Giroux in August, 1994.

Dennis Hopper is an actor, director, photographer, and painter. The movies he has directed include *Easy Rider, Colors, The Hot Spot,* and most recently *Chasers.* Exhibitions of his visual work have been held in Barcelona, Paris, Boston, New York, and Los Angeles.

Stokes Howell has published stories in *Sulfur, Exquisite Corpse, Tales of the Heart,* and other magazines. He is currently completing a volume of short stories, writing a film version of *Tristan and Isolde* for Brazilian director Gerald Thomas, and creating an opera libretto for German composer Peter Eotvos.

Darius James is the author of *Negrophobia, The Fourth Coming,* and *That's Blaxploitation!!!* (forthcoming from St. Martin's Press), from which his interview with Melvin Van Peebles is excerpted. He has written for *Spin, Penthouse,* and *Puritan.* He lives in Brooklyn, New York.

Mike Kelley's work was the subject of a recent survey at the Whitney Museum of American Art that also traveled to Los Angeles and Stockholm. In 1993, he organized and contributed the catalogue essay (from which his notes on Forrest J Ackerman are excerpted) for "The Uncanny," a group exhibition at the Gemeentemuseum in Arnhem, the Netherlands. Born in Detroit in 1954, he lives and works in Los Angeles.

Robert Kensinger is a production designer living in Hollywood.

August Kleinzahler lives in San Francisco, a three-hour drive from Reno. His most recent collection of poetry, *Earthquake Weather*, was published by Moyer Bell. He is the recipient of a Lila Wallace–Reader's Digest fellowship and works with homeless veterans in San Francisco's Tenderloin district.

Damon Krukowski's work recently appeared in *Oblek 12: Writing from the New Coast* and in *The Impercipient*. He also has work forthcoming in *Tyuonyi*. He is the editor of Exact Change, a small press that specializes in reprints of Surrealist fiction, and a sometime rock musician with a Robert Wyatt fixation.

James Laughlin's "The Desert in Bloom" is a segment from his long poem-in-progress, *Byways*. His collected poems have recently been published by Moyer Bell.

Robert Mahoney is an art critic who has regularly contributed to *Arts*, *Flash Art*, *Sculpture*, and *C*. He is the author of *Bruce Hellander: Curious Collage*, recently published by Grassfield Press. He lives in New York.

Kristine McKenna is a Los Angeles–based writer who covers the arts. Her work has appeared in the *Los Angeles Times*, the *New York Times*, *Rolling Stone*, and *ARTnews*.

Hilda Morley is the author of several books of poetry, most recently *Between the Rocks*, published in a limited, fine-press edition by Tangram Press. She has received Guggenheim, New York State Foundation for the Arts, and other grants. Her book *To Hold in My Hand* received the first Capricorn Award. She is currently working on a biographical memoir of her late husband, the composer Stefan Wolpe.

Martin Paul and **José A. Elgorriaga** teach at California State University, Fresno. Their translations have appeared in the *American Poetry Review*, *Ironwood*, *Mundus Artium*, and the *Portland Review*. Their book, *The Other Shore: 100 Poems of Rafael Alberti*, was published in 1981.

CONTRIBUTORS

Tom Paulin's new book of poems, *Walking a Line*, is published by Faber & Faber. A collection of critical essays, *Minotaur*, including essays on Emily Dickinson, Robert Frost, and Elizabeth Bishop, was published by Harvard University Press in 1992. He is a professor of poetry at the University of Nottingham.

Iva Pekárková was born in 1963 in Prague. She spent a year in an Austrian refugee camp before coming to the United States in 1986. The author of *Truck Stop Rainbows*, she divides her time between Prague and driving a cab in New York City. Her novel, *The World is Round*, from which her story of the same name is adapted, will be published by Farrar, Straus & Giroux in August, 1994.

Raymond Pettibon was born in Tucson, Arizona, in 1957. His work has been included in the 1993 Whitney Biennial and the seminal group exhibition "Helter Skelter: L.A. Art in the 1990s" at the Museum of Contemporary Art in Los Angeles. Recent solo exhibitions have been held at Galerie Metropol, Vienna, David Zwirner and Feature Gallery, New York, and Galeria Massimo de Carlo, Milan. He lives and works in Hermosa Beach, California.

David Powelstock is the translator of Iva Pekárková's first novel, *Truck Stop Rainbows*, as well as of other Czech and Russian poetry and prose. He will be assistant professor of Slavic Languages and Literature at the University of Chicago as of September, 1994.

Edward Ruscha was born in Omaha, Nebraska, in 1937. His first solo exhibition was held at the Ferus Gallery, Los Angeles, in 1963. His recent solo museum exhibitions include those at the Musée National d'Art Moderne, Paris, the Whitney Museum of American Art, New York, the Museum of Contemporary Art, Los Angeles, and the Serpentine Gallery, London. He lives and works in Los Angeles.

Terry Southern's novels include *Flash and Filigree*, *The Magic Christian*, *Blue Movie*, *Candy* (with Mason Hoffenberg), and, most recently, *Texas Summer*. His screeplays include *Barbarella*, *Dr. Strangelove*, and *Easy Rider*.

Quentin Tarantino's screenplays include *True Romance*, directed by Tony Scott, and *Natural Born Killers*, directed by Oliver Stone, which will be released in the summer of 1994. Tarantino wrote and directed *Reservoir Dogs* (1992) and *Pulp Fiction*, which Miramax will release in August, 1994.

CONTRIBUTORS

John Tranter is an Australian poet who has worked in publishing and radio production. Ten collections of his verse have appeared, the most recent of which are *Under Berlin* and *At the Florida* (University of Queensland Press). He recently edited, with Philip Mead, the *Penguin Book of Modern Australian Poetry*.

Melvin Van Peebles is a writer, songwriter, film director, actor, and producer. His films include *Watermelon Man* and *Sweet Sweetback's Baadasssss Song*. His musicals include *Ain't Supposed to Die a Natural Death* and *Becky*. He is currently recording a new album (which will include the song "Just Dont Make Sense") and co-producing a movie chronicling the Black Panther Party.

Krishna Winston is a professor of German and acting dean at Wesleyan University who has translated the work of Golo Mann, Günter Grass, Christoph Hein, and Siegfried Lenz.

In *Grand Street* 48 **Agha Shahid Ali**'s name was inadvertently misspelled.

We apologize for an omission in *Grand Street* 48. **Charles Palliser**'s "The Medicine Man" is an excerpt from his book *Betrayals* to be published in the spring of 1995 by Ballantine.

TRAPPED IN A WHIRLWIND OF DISBELIEF, I REACHED OUT AND GRABBED THE NEAREST MYTH I COULD FIND, STEADYING MYSELF FOR A BRIEF MOMENT.

Statement of Ownership

Statement of Ownership, Management, and Circulation (Act of August 12, 1970: Section 3685. Title 39. United States Code). No. 1. Title of Publication: Grand Street. No. 2. Date of filing: 12-31-93. No. 3. Frequency of issue: quarterly. No. 4. Location of the known office of publication: 131 Varick Street, Room 906, New York, N.Y. 10013. No. 5. Location of the headquarters or general business offices of the publisher: 131 Varick Street, Room 906, New York, N.Y. 10013. No. 6. Name and address of publisher and editor: Jean Stein, 131 Varick Street, Room 906, New York, N.Y. 10013. No. 7. Owner: New York Foundation for the Arts, 155 Ave. of the Americas, New York, N.Y. 10013-1507. No. 8. Known bondholders, mortgagees, and other security holders owning or holding one percent or more of the total amount of bonds, mortgages, or other securities: none. No. 9. For optional completion by publishers mailing at regular rates. No. 10. Extent and nature of circulation. Average number of copies each issue during preceding twelve months. No. A. Total number of copies printed: 7,000. No. B. Paid circulation: 1. Sales through dealers and carriers, street vendors, and counter sales: 2,910. 2. Mail subscriptions: 1,014. No. C. Total paid circulation: 3,924. No. D. Free distribution by mail, carrier, or other means: 525. No. E. Total distribution: 4,449. No. F. Copies not distributed: 1. Office use, left over, unaccounted, spoiled after printing: 2,239. 2. Returned from news agents: 312. No. G. Total: 7000. Actual number of copies of single issue published nearest to filing date: 7,000. No. 11. I certify that the statements made by me above are correct and complete. Signature of editor, publisher, business manager, or owner: Jean Stein, editor and publisher.

ILLUSTRATIONS

front & back cover William Eggleston, two untitled photographs, 1994, Ektacolor print from 35mm color negative, 8 x 10 in. Courtesy of the artist and Andra Eggleston.

title page William Eggleston, *Untitled* (detail), 1994, Ektacolor print from 35mm color negative, 8 x 10 in. Courtesy of the artist and Andra Eggleston.

pp. 10, 15, 18, 19, 22 Dennis Hopper, eight untitled photographs with text, 1994, paint marker on silver gelatin print, 8 x 10 in. each. Courtesy of the artist.

pp. 25–32 Georganne Deen, seven works. Courtesy of the artist.

p. 25 *My Diet Pill Is Wearin' Off*, 1989, gouache on paper, 23 x 15 in. Collection of Danny Elfman.

p. 26 *The Single-minded Pursuit Of More*, 1986, oil on canvas, 30 x 40 in. Collection of Margaret Johnson.

p. 27 *The Wheel Of Misfortune*, 1994, gouache on paper, 17 x 13 in.

pp. 28–29 *Weeping Women Of Hollywood*, 1994, pencil and gouache on paper, 15 x 10 in.

p. 30 *Venus D'Hollywood (Model)*, 1994, gouache on paper, 14 x 11½ in.

p. 31 *Venus D'Hollywood (Actress)*, 1992, gouache on paper, 13½ x 10 in.

p. 32 *The Connoisseur*, 1983, mixed media, 14 x 11 in. Collection of Margaret Johnson.

pp. 49–63 William Eggleston, fifteen untitled photographs, 1994, Ektacolor prints from 35mm color negatives, 8 x 10 in. each. Courtesy of the artist and Andra Eggleston.

p. 64 Original studio publicity for the motion picture *Dr. Strangelove*. Courtesy of Terry Southern and Gail Gerber.

p. 75 Peter Sellers in *Dr. Strangelove*. Photograph courtesy of the Bettmann Archive.

p. 80 "War Room" scene from *Dr. Strangelove*. Photograph courtesy of the Bettmann Archive.

p. 95 Original dust jacket for the first edition of *Other Voices, Other Rooms* by Truman Capote. Courtesy of Hilton Als.

pp. 96–97 (background) Harold Halma, *Truman Capote*, 1948. Photograph courtesy of Random House.

p. 105 Eudora Welty, *Katherine Anne Porter At Yaddo*, 1940. Photograph courtesy of the Eudora Welty Collection, Mississippi Department of Archives and History.

p. 106 Karl Bissinger, *Jane Bowles*, 1946. Photograph courtesy of Karl Bissinger.

pp. 113–20 Edward Ruscha, seven works (titles and dates appear on p.112). Courtesy of the artist and Leo Castelli Gallery, New York.

p. 113 Acrylic on linen, 20 x 24 in.

p. 114 Acrylic on paper, 24 x 30 in.

p. 115 Acrylic on paper, 24 x 30 in.

pp. 116–17 Acrylic on canvas, 34 x 72 in.

p. 118 Acrylic on paper, 24 x 30 in.

p. 119 Acrylic on paper, 24 x 30 in.

p. 120 Acrylic and pigmented varnish on canvas, 40 x 72 in.

p. 150 Photograph of Melvin Van Peebles. Courtesy of the Bettmann Archive.

pp. 155, 159 Scenes from the motion picture *Sweet Sweetback's Baadasssss Song*. Photographs courtesy of Photofest.

pp. 161–70 Raymond Pettibon, eleven untitled drawings. Courtesy of the artist and Feature Gallery, New York.

p. 161 1990, ink and mixed media on paper, 11¼ x 9 in.

p. 162 1989, ink and mixed media on paper, 14 x 11 in.

p. 163 1992, ink on paper, 11 x 8½ in.

p. 164 1990, ink and mixed media on paper, 14 x 11 in.

p. 165 1990, ink on paper, 22 x 17 in.

p. 166 1991, ink on paper, 18½ x 11 in.

p. 167 1990, ink on paper, 15 x 9¾ in.

p. 168 1985, ink on paper, 14 x 11 in.

p. 169 1989, ink on paper, 14 x 11 in.

p. 170 (top) 1986, ink on paper, 14 x 11 in.

p. 170 (bottom) 1991, ink on paper, 11¼ x 9 in.

p. 188 Photograph by Harry Langdon Jr. Courtesy of The Douris Corporation.

pp. 197–198, 201 (top right), **204–5** (bottom), and **207** Courtesy of the Academy of Motion Picture Arts and Sciences.

pp. 199 (top) and **202** (bottom) Courtesy of Peter Brosnan.

pp. 199 (center and bottom), **200** (bottom), **200–01** (background), and **201** (center and bottom) Courtesy of Robert Birchard.

pp. 202–3 (background), **203** (top), **205** (center right), and **206** (bottom right) Photographs by Kelvin Jones. Courtesy of Kelvin Jones.

p. 203 (bottom) Courtesy of John Parker.

pp. 204 (center left) and **206** (top left) photographs by Edward S. Curtis. Courtesy of the California Historical Society, San Francisco.

pp. 204 (top right) and **205** (top and center left) Photographs by Gray Crawford.

pp. 225–33 Daniel Faust, fourteen untitled photographs, November 1993, Cibachrome prints from Kodachrome slides, dimensions variable. Courtesy of the artist and American Fine Arts, Co., New York.

p. 235 Courtesy of Special Collections, Library of the University of California at Santa Barbara.

pp. 236, 243, 246 Courtesy of Robert Kensinger.

p. 261 Posted in lower Manhattan, April 1994.

FOUND
O B J E C T

A JOURNAL OF ART, THEORY AND CULTURAL STUDIES FROM THE CENTER FOR CULTURAL STUDIES, CUNY GRADUATE CENTER

ISSUE 3 (SPRING 1994)

Jürgen Habermas
on Utopian Politics in a Multicultural Society

Noam Chomsky
on the Israel-Arafat Agreement

Jonathan Boyarin
on Palestinian Ruins in Israel

Vincent Crapanzano
on Boyarin

Special Section
The Politics of Peace in the Middle East:

Joel Beinin and Joseph Massad critique the peace process

Meena Alexander
Fault Lines: Selection from a Memoir

With art by:
Jessica Diamond

SUBSCRIBE TO FOUND OBJECT

INDIVIDUAL:

☐ SINGLE ISSUE: $5.00 ($7.00 overseas) ISSUE NUMBER:_____

☐ SUBSCRIPTION RATE: 3 issues for $12.00 ($18.00 overseas)

START WITH ISSUE: _____

INSTITUTIONAL:

☐ SINGLE ISSUE: $10.00 ($12.00 overseas) ISSUE NUMBER:_____

☐ SUBSCRIPTION RATE: 3 issues for $27.00 ($33.00 overseas)

START WITH ISSUE: _____

(Order now and get Issue One free)

ADDRESS:
name:_____

street:_____

_____

city:_____

state:_____ zip:_____

(Make Check Payable to The Center for Cultural Studies)

Found Object, %o Center for Cultural Studies
CUNY Graduate Center 33 West 42nd Street New York, NY 10036

That we descant and yet again descant

Upon the supreme theme of Art and Song . . .

Speech after long silence; it is right, . . .

W. B. Yeats After Long Silence 1931

descant

a literary and arts journal of distinction

---

subscriptions: p.o. box 314, station p, toronto, canada m5s 2s8
twenty six canadian dollars, one person, one year

MARK RUDMAN

Rider

Rider takes the poetry of autobiography, with its scenes of instruction, to a new plane. In a polyphonic narrative that combines verse with lyrical prose and often humorous dialogue, Mark Rudman examines his own coming-of-age through the lens of his relationships with his grandfather, father, step-father, and son and against the background of a family history anchored in the traditions of Judaism and the culture of the diaspora.

"Relationships and characterizations are unfolded with brilliant boldness. It is striking the way this work evolves into a moving elegy in this brave, very American work . . . A new departure."

— M. L. ROSENTHAL

Praise for Mark Rudman's other books of poetry . . .

"Rudman displays considerable craftsmanship and control over his material as he confronts a complex world with a sensitivity that is acute, subtle, and entirely unshielded."

— LESLIE ULLMAN, *New York Times Book Review*

"Here is a poetry that has a chance of seeing the world . . . the public poetry of a private person, inheritor but radical transmutor of the legacies of so diverse a pair as Walt Whitman and Robert Lowell."

— ROGER MITCHELL, *American Book Review*

$22.50 cloth / $10.95 paper

WESLEYAN POETRY

New England

University Press of New England • Hanover, NH 03755-2048 • 800-421-1561

Belles Lettres
A Review Of Books By Women
• •
A Quarterly Magazine Of Interviews, Essays, Candid Columns, & International Book News

Whenever *Belles Lettres* arrives in the mail, it's like greeting a trusted, thoughtful, and well-travelled friend who is going to tell me the books I most want and need to read. Its reviews connect women's writings to their traditions, criticize in a way that helps writers make our work better, and always remember that women's ideas must stand the test of women's experience. —Gloria Steinem

• • • • • • • • • • • •

Belles Lettres is the most exciting thing that has arrived in my mailbox since my refund from the IRS. My own career would have still been assigned to the hinterlands of "maybe" had it not been for my discovery of a single text by a woman writer who reflected my existence. How wonderful to think that such a feast awaits other women and men in need of a balanced perspective of the richness existing in American and world literature. —Gloria Naylor

Annual subscription $20 (4 issues); sample $3
P.O. Box 372068, Dept. 27, Satellite Beach, FL 32937-0068

Name

Address   City, State, Zip Code

An Indispensable Collection

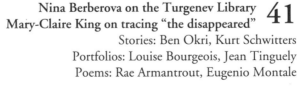

Back Issues of Grand Street

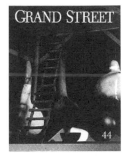

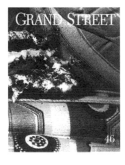
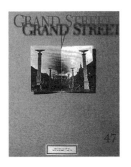

Now Available–
Order Them While They Last

CALL 1-800-807-6548 or send name, address, issue number(s), and quantity.
American Express, Mastercard, and Visa accepted; please send credit card number and expiration
date. Payment must be in U.S. dollars. Back issues are $12.00 each ($15.00 overseas and
Canada), which includes postage and handling.
Address orders to *Grand Street* Back Issues, 131 Varick Street, Suite 906, New York, N.Y. 10013.

Trafika

An International Literary Review

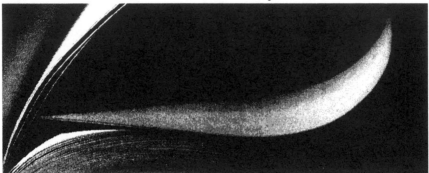

Trafika is a new international literary review for the contemporary poetry, fiction, and essays of established and emerging writers from throughout the world.
Published quarterly in Prague and distributed internationally, *Trafika* maintains a special commitment to introducing, in translation, the works of non-English-language writers to a worldwide audience.

Subscription rates 4 issues annually

individual subscription:	US $35
institutional subscription:	US $40
sample copy:	US $10

Shipping & handling included

Please send check, money order or credit card # (VISA, AMEX or EUROCARD/MasterCard, including expiration date and signature) to:

All Other Countries:	US & Canada:
Trafika	*Trafika*
Janovského 14	P.O. Box 446
170 00 Prague 7	Canoga Park, CA
Czech Republic	91305 USA